SUDDENLY TWO PISTOLS ROARED ALMOST TOGETHER...

The gunman's body jerked under the impact of a bullet, and his own shot went wild, gouging splinters out of the deck only inches from Raider's head.

Rolling to his feet, Raider saw Dick standing farther back along the deck, a smoking pistol in his hand. "I decided to come up on deck," Dick said apologetically.

Raider looked over at the dead gunman, then at the place where the gunman's bullet had hit. He remembered waiting for that bullet to plow into his body. He turned toward Dick and shrugged. "Hell...I ain't complainin'."

Other books in the RAIDER Series by
J.D. HARDIN

RAIDER
SIXGUN CIRCUS
THE YUMA ROUNDUP
THE GUNS OF EL DORADO
THIRST FOR VENGEANCE
DEATH'S DEAL
VENGEANCE RIDE
CHEYENNE FRAUD
THE GULF PIRATES
TIMBER WAR
SILVER CITY AMBUSH

THE
NORTHWEST
RAILROAD WAR

BERKLEY BOOKS, NEW YORK

THE NORTHWEST RAILROAD WAR

A Berkley Book/published by arrangement with
the author

PRINTING HISTORY
Berkley edition/June 1988

All rights reserved.
Copyright © 1988 by J.D. Hardin
This book may not be reproduced in whole or in part,
by mimeograph or any other means, without permission.
For information address: The Berkley Publishing Group,
200 Madison Avenue, New York, NY 10016.

ISBN: 0-425-10890-2

A BERKLEY BOOK ® TM 757,375
Berkley Books are published by the Berkley Publishing Group,
200 Madison Avenue, New York, NY 10016
The name "BERKLEY" and the "B" logo
are trademarks belonging to the Berkley Publishing Corporation.

PRINTED IN THE UNITED STATES OF AMERICA

10 9 8 7 6 5 4 3 2 1

CHAPTER ONE

As usual, the road was muddy, the gluey stuff sucking at Michael Haney's boots as he walked toward the big two-story house that dominated the little town. It was actually more construction camp than town. Many of the buildings were temporary clapboard affairs: warehouses, offices, bunkhouses for laborers—most of these latter empty now that work had finally progressed so much farther up the line.

Fort Yale, British Columbia, an isolated outpost of empire. The Fraser River ran by the front of the town. A stern-wheel steamboat was tied up at the rickety dock. High mountains rose immediately behind the settled area, the slopes heavily forested, except for large bare areas where the trees had been cut for lumber to build the town —and to satisfy the voracious appetite of the new railroad for trestles, snow sheds, ties, and housing for the thousands of men working to build it.

The boss's house always impressed Haney. It seemed so substantial in comparison to the rest of Yale's buildings—

substantial like its owner, Andrew Onderdonk. Haney was always a little nervous when he approached the house. It was one thing to meet Onderdonk at the work sites, another to see him at home. Onderdonk had always made Haney somewhat ill at ease. The man never really *said* much of anything. So damned reticent, even when he gave a party or a reception at the house, which he did often. His wife saw to that.

Haney was clumping up the steps when Onderdonk himself came out onto the big front veranda. Dressed to the nines as usual, Haney noticed. A suit, a real suit in all this mud and dirt; his shirt fresh, starched, and very white; a foulard tie at his throat; his boots cleaned and polished. One hell of a good-looking bastard, Haney thought a little enviously. Just touching forty years old, tall, strapping, erect carriage, a fine straight nose and high forehead under curly hair parted in the middle. His beard was parted in the middle too, thick and curly and brown. But it was his eyes that were his most compelling feature, fine and bright, calm and clear. Haney himself was good-looking enough, fairly tall, if not as tall as Onderdonk, with a roundish face and huge handlebar mustache that made him look a little like an Irish version of Lord Kitchener.

"Good morning, Haney," Onderdonk said in his usual quiet, polite manner.

"Morning, A.O. Ready for the trip?"

Onderdonk's eyebrows rose slightly. "Of course I am. Shall we start out?"

It was not really a question, and Onderdonk immediately stepped off the veranda down into that muddy horror of a road. Haney took a quick look back at the house, saw that Mrs. Onderdonk was standing just inside the front door, a short, somewhat plump blond woman, a little younger than her husband.

She smiled her usual radiant smile. "Good morning, Michael."

"Morning, ma'am."

A quick lifting of his hat, and Haney set out after Onderdonk, who was already twenty yards ahead. As Haney stepped off the veranda he looked back once more at Mrs. Onderdonk. She was dressed in her habitual sober, simple attire. Her husband was the family's only real clotheshorse.

Haney soon caught up to his boss. He glanced down at Onderdonk's boots. Goddamn! How did the man do it? Onderdonk's boots were practically as clean as when he'd come out onto the veranda, while Haney's looked like big balls of mud. Nothing seemed to stick to Onderdonk, not mud, nor dust, nor even, apparently, worry. Although the man had plenty of worry about.

It was not a long walk to the rail line. The train was waiting, a short one, consisting only of an engine, a wood tender, and two flatcars, one of them outfitted with seats. Already some section heads and other brass were waiting. This particular train was slated for an inspection trip. Andrew Onderdonk was going to take a close look at what had become the biggest project of his already rather distinguished career as an engineer and builder—the British Columbia section of the new Canadian Pacific transcontinental railroad.

After a nodding of heads, a few terse greetings—Onderdonk was being his usual taciturn self—the engineer hauled on his lanyard, the engine's whistle shrieked, venting a plume of steam, and a moment later the car couplings clanged, the train jerked forward, then back, then forward again, and they were under way.

Haney surreptitiously studied Onderdonk as the train attacked the first grade up into the mountains. As usual Onderdonk was sitting quietly, cool as a cucumber, looking very much like the Duke of Something-or-other. Well, why shouldn't he? Haney wondered what he himself would have been like if he'd had Onderdonk's advantages, if he had come from an old New York family, like Onderdonk's, so old a family that Onderdonk was descended from the Dutch settlers who had preceded the English in settling New York State. Onderdonk had grown up with money, and position, and a sense of knowing exactly who and what he was. Haney had long ago detected in the other man an unquestioning knowledge of his role in life. A role right up there at the top.

Which constituted a considerable difference from Haney's background of struggling Irish immigrants. He'd come a long way from that background; hell, he was Onderdonk's right-hand man, Mr. Number Two on what was probably the greatest engineering feat of the century. He knew, though, that plenty of rough edges still clung to him, that he would never, in all his life, have that certainty, that calm sense of security exhibited by Andrew Onderdonk.

Well, so what? Haney knew that many of the men didn't like him, that they resented his manner, the way he gave orders. He himself wouldn't have put it that way, but Michael Haney had a big, loud, Irish mouth. He was a pusher—which was why he had the job he had. And if a big loud mouth was what it took to keep that fucking construction rabble moving, he'd just keep on shouting.

Despite his genius as an engineer, Andrew Onderdonk was not a detail man, not the best of administrators. When construction had been flagging a year ago, when money was flowing out so fast it looked like there wouldn't be enough to finish Onderdonk's portion of the railroad, Haney had been called onto the scene. And he'd made it all work right. Efficiency. That was Michael Haney's motto. And it was undoubtedly part of the reason for some of the anger directed his way. He'd had to step on toes, break up careless habits, change the way men did things. But Haney's changes had for the most part worked, and now the line was moving again, building more rapidly up through those awesome mountains. They now had a chance to finish the work on time.

The train steamed higher and higher, toward the first of the tunnels that took the track through the mountains. Onderdonk, still sitting quietly, studied the landscape, remembering those first agonizing years of construction, when men hung by ropes down sheer granite cliffs, drilling blast holes into the rock to start the tunnels. It had taken eighteen months to lay the first two miles of track east of Yale. Two years in all for the first twenty miles. And at what a cost, in dollars, in sweat, and most of all, in men —lives lost, bodies mangled. What boldness it must have taken to even imagine the building of a railroad through such incredibly rugged country. He admired the courage, the vision of those early planners, but of course, it was going to be up to him to make it a reality. Digging, blasting through those mountains. When his part of the road was finished, there'd be twenty-seven tunnels gouged out of that hard, unforgiving granite.

If he did finish. If the job didn't break him financially. The early delays, the higher-than-expected freight costs, the difficulty in finding and hiring good men, it had all hurt. Thank God for the Chinese. They could outwork the average spoiled white man; certainly they could outwork the trash he'd had shipped up from San Francisco. He'd brought Cantonese coolies across the Pacific in ship after ship, thousands of them. He knew that didn't make him popular with the local whites. Too bad. He had a railroad to build.

The train crossed a trestle. Not one of the temporary wooden ones, but an iron trestle. Things were progressing. A little way ahead, the rails cut through a shoulder of the mountain, just for a hundred feet or so. Below the cut, the mountain fell away for hundreds of yards, straight down.

The train reached the first real tunnel. The men were suddenly separated from one another by darkness, each with his own thoughts. Haney was wondering how he could boost production in the local explosives factory he had built. Onderdonk was thinking darkly of the latest troubles, the accidents, the problems with the men, things that should not be happening the way they were happening. He and Haney were alone in their musings. Most of the other men were laughing and joking, their burden of responsibility correspondingly lighter.

The train went in and out of tunnels, light, then dark, then light again. Finally, after more than an hour, end of track lay just ahead. The train was stopped well back, because, as usual, blasting was under way. The men dismounted from the cars and walked ahead. Haney noticed that, as usual, very little of the engine soot had stuck to Onderdonk. What the hell was the man made of?

They were stopped by a crew boss just as they were about to round a bend. "Fire in the hole," he said tersely. Onderdonk pushed past him, standing close to the angle of an outcropping, but still partially in the open. Haney came up beside him. The ragged mouth of tunnel gaped blackly about two hundred yards ahead. Most of the men in sight were hunched down behind boulders or outcroppings, staring down at the ground as they waited for the blast. Haney stiffened angrily. "What the hell are those wagons doing out there in the open?" he shouted, pointing toward three freight wagons, still hitched to their teams.

He had no chance to say anything else. A thunderous roar burst from deep inside the throat of the tunnel. The ground shook beneath them. A moment later a huge cloud of dust billowed out of the tunnel's mouth, and slightly ahead of the dust two huge boulders arced through the air, blown out of the tunnel like cannonballs out of a giant gun.

One of the boulders plowed into a stretch of forest, cutting a swath through the trees. The other struck one of the wagons. Wood splinters flew into the air, horses screamed, blood and flesh sprayed everywhere.

Men started to run toward the wrecked wagon. A crew boss, shouting at the top of his lungs, called them back. Sure enough, a secondary explosion went off deep inside the tunnel. More debris shot out of the tunnel mouth, but nothing as destructive as those two huge boulders.

Now men ran to the wagons. Three horses were down, one dead, its head completely missing, the other two horribly mangled. One man produced a pistol. The short flat crack of pistol shots rang out. The horses stopped struggling and screaming. Haney ran forward. "I want the man responsible for leaving these wagons out here in the open," he shouted, taking one man by the arm.

The man angrily shrugged him off. "It sure as hell wasn't me."

"Who, then? Because he's sure as hell finished with this outfit."

"It's Ben Abercrombie," someone else said. "Those are his wagons."

"Then where is he?"

The man who had spoken shrugged. "Over behind those rocks. Drunk, I guess."

"Drunk? Where the hell'd he get the whiskey? I've given orders..."

Onderdonk strolled away, leaving it to Haney to handle what had to be done. It was what he'd been hired for. There had been a lot of this kind of thing lately. More than would seem natural. He wondered what he could do about it. Wondered if he wasn't perhaps imagining it all. Perhaps it was only normal, this sudden rash of accidents, the disaffection among the men. Perhaps his own discomfort, the financial strain, was making him imagine things.

Now that the blasting was over, the train came chuffing slowly around the outcropping it had stopped behind, then came to a halt about fifty yards ahead of Onderdonk. The track here lay more or less in the open, with the river nearly two hundred feet below, on the left, down a relatively gentle slope. Two hundred yards ahead, the blank granite face of the mountain rose nearly straight up, the smooth stone broken only by the black maw of the tunnel opening, which, from this distance, looked as if it were painted onto the rock. That's the way it had been from the beginning—tunnel, open space, tunnel, open space, ad nauseum.

The land climbed steeply to Onderdonk's right, above the track, a slope reaching up about three hundred feet, made up partly of rock, partly of earth. Scattered granite outcroppings were all that was holding the slope in place. A potentially dangerous situation. Later, something would have to be done to protect the open track below.

Onderdonk became aware of why his attention had been

drawn to this slope. A thin trickle of dirt and rock was sliding downhill. He looked up. Was that a man up there, at the very top? Haney was walking toward Onderdonk, his Irish face still mottled red with anger. Onderdonk pointed upward. Haney looked up and saw the man. "What the hell is he doing?" Haney started to say. The man was clambering up from an outcropping of shaly rock. To the experienced eyes of both men, it was clear that the outcropping held the entire slope together.

And then they both saw it, the thin plume of blue smoke spiraling up into the air from just below the outcropping. "Fire in the hole!" Haney shouted. Everywhere men looked up, wondering if another explosion was hanging fire inside the tunnel.

And then the earth erupted beneath the outcropping. Dirt and rocks shot into the air. The outcropping held for a second or two, then slowly began to slide downslope. The mass of earth and stone above trembled, then followed, moving majestically, slowly gathering speed, roaring down toward the rail line and the men below.

Haney had grabbed Onderdonk's arm and was dragging him back toward the place where they'd sheltered from the previous blast. Onderdonk made it just in time; several boulders crashed by, pulverizing the spot where he'd been standing only a second or two before. Both he and Haney crouched behind cover, watching as the huge earth slide plowed into the right side of the train. For a moment it looked as if the train would stay on the tracks, as if it would form a dam and stop the surging tide of dirt and rocks, but the vast weight of it was too much, and the train, buckling toward the center, was forced off the tracks. It hung for a moment, steam spouting from the broken boiler, then tumbled down the slope into the river below, followed by the earth slide.

Thirty seconds later it was all over. An enormous dust cloud hung over the river gorge, obscuring the train, although there could be little doubt that it was buried under hundreds of tons of debris. There was dust everywhere, and now Onderdonk's neat clothing was no longer quite so neat. Haney rushed by him, heading toward the place where the train had gone over. Nothing was left there now; the tracks were completely buried deep beneath the earth slide, pieces of tree and rock thrusting up out of the mess.

Haney noticed that Onderdonk was lagging behind, and, turning, he saw him staring up at the slope above. "There he goes," Onderdonk said in his usual quiet, well-modulated voice. Haney looked up. He saw the man again, now all the way at the top of the slope, lead a horse out of the trees, leap onto its back, and gallop away. The distance was too great to make out any features. "The son of a bitch!" Haney screamed. "I'll have his guts for garters! Careless bastard!"

Onderdonk shook his head. "Not careless at all, Haney. I think he did his job very well."

"What? You mean he... It was..."

"Sabotage, Haney. I wasn't certain before, but now I am."

He looked from the top of the slope to Haney, then back up the slope again. "And now that I'm certain, something will definitely be done about it," he stated, his normally imperturbable face reflecting more emotion than Haney had ever seen there before.

CHAPTER TWO

The big blond reached across Raider's naked torso and pinched the skin around his midriff. "You're getting fat," she said accusingly.

Raider responded by cupping one of her breasts. "So are you, Mae. This part of you, anyhow. But I ain't complainin'."

"I'm serious. It's all this sitting around, or rather," Mae added with a quick giggle, "all this lying around. All the eating and drinking. You guzzle beer like a man who just crawled out of the desert after a month of hard times."

"I *like* beer," Raider said lazily, shifting his hand to the blond's other breast.

She shivered with pleasure. "What you really need," she said huskily, "is more exercise. Lots of exercise. Something that'll make you work up a real sweat."

"What you got in mind?" he asked, grinning.

"What the hell do you think?" she replied, her voice even more husky.

Raider and Mae were sprawled on a large bed on the

THE NORTHWEST RAILROAD WAR 11

second floor of the finest whorehouse in San Antonio. Raider was wearing only his trousers. A filmy peignoir did very little to cover Mae's voluptuous body. Large, firm, pink-nippled breasts spilled out the front of the peignoir, which was slowly slipping further down the girl's torso, until only the swell of her hips was holding it up. Raider shifted his hand from Mae's breasts and pushed the peignoir down even further. Now a few wispy tendrils of blond fur showed, about four inches below her navel. "Yeah... maybe you're right, Mae," he murmured. "Maybe I could use a little exercise."

"And you won't even have to get out of bed."

Mae began fumbling with Raider's belt buckle, while Raider, having a little trouble with the clinging folds of the peignoir, was trying to unwrap it from around the girl's thighs. Undoubtedly they would have both eventually succeeded in their attempts to disrobe one another, and undoubtedly Raider would have got his exercise, had it not been for the interruption. They were both breathing rather heavily, Raider preparing to roll Mae over onto her back while at the same time trying to kick his trousers off his left foot, when there was a sudden commotion from downstairs.

"Oh, goddamn it," Raider growled.

"Don't pay any attention to it," Mae panted, pulling him down onto her.

"Well, maybe if it don't get any worse...."

But the sound of shouting downstairs intensified. "Sir, you can't go up there," a woman's voice called out sharply. The voice belonged to Livonia, the woman who owned this particular establishment.

"The hell I can't," a man's voice bellowed back. "I know damn well he's up there. The word's out all over town—hell, all over the state—that he's up there. Raider!" the voice bellowed. "Get your ass down here, or I'm coming on up!"

Raider groaned. He recognized the man's voice. It belonged to James McParland, head of the Denver office of the Pinkerton National Detective Agency. He knew McParland well enough to realize that he'd do whatever he said he'd do, even if that meant coming upstairs and hauling him off Mae's naked body.

Raider started to roll himself out of bed.

"Goddamn it," Mae said bitterly. "Some days nothing at all goes right."

As he headed toward the door, Raider looked back at the girl. She lay on her back on the bed, totally naked, a breathtaking vision of blond hair, blue eyes, pink flesh in lush abundance, and, of course, all that marvelous lust literally leaking from her. Goddamned troublemaking McParland!

He opened the door a crack. "Okay, McParland. I'm on my way down. Just quit that goddamned yellin'. Jesus. You'd think you was brought up in a barn."

"Well, I sure as hell wasn't brought up in any whorehouse," McParland shouted back.

"Watch your mouth!" both Raider and Livonia called out together.

Raider slammed the door and stepped back into the room, heading for his clothes. Mae had propped herself up on one elbow and was looking at him admiringly. Lord above, but he was one hell of a fine-looking man!

Raider was big, over six feet tall, broad-shouldered, lean-hipped, rawhide tough. His body was crisscrossed by scars from old bullet and knife wounds. Mae felt a thrill every time she saw those scars, and an even bigger thrill every time she had a chance to run her hands over them. She sighed as Raider pulled on his pants and shirt, covering up all that maleness. Not that his face wasn't worth looking at—tanned skin, black hair, a thick black mustache curving down around the sides of his mouth, and hard snapping black eyes. His face was as lean and strong as the rest of him.

Raider sat down in the room's only chair—the bed took up most of the available space—and pulled on his boots. Nice handmade boots, she noticed, even if they looked like they'd been run over by a forty-mule-team freight wagon. Still naked, the girl watched him head for the doorway, his boots clumping loudly against the scarred wooden floor. He turned at the door and looked back at her. "Don't you go nowhere," he said. "I'll be back."

As he went out into the hall, she smiled after him, hoping that he'd be able to keep his word. Who the hell was that man downstairs, anyhow? He'd sure riled Raider; she'd never seen him this upset. He'd even forgotten to take his pistol. The big Remington was still in its holster, hanging by its belt from the bedpost. First time she'd seen it out of his reach. Well, maybe that was good. He'd eventually come back for it, that was for certain. She'd just lie here, and wait, and think dirty thoughts.

Raider clumped down the stairs, doing a slow boil. Reaching the ground floor, he walked into the parlor. Miss Livonia had decorated the place in the best Texas whorehouse style, plush materials everywhere, big glittering chandeliers, oceans of purples and reds, and lots of glass gleaming behind the big mahogany bar. Miss Livonia's customers never had any doubt that this was the big time, as far as whorehouses went.

Livonia strode up to Raider. She was about forty-five years old, with long thick dark hair and nice eyes. She had probably been one hell of a looker ten or fifteen years and a hundred pounds ago, when she was still a simple working girl, but now, whenever she moved, she looked like a walking earthquake. She sailed up to Raider, regal as a battleship, her eyes snapping angrily. "Really," she snapped. "Really, Raider, the kind of friends that come looking for you . . ."

Raider looked past her, to the man standing in the middle of the parlor. "I wouldn't exactly call him a friend," he growled.

McParland headed toward him, taking the great-circle route around Miss Livonia. McParland was not exactly small himself, a tall, somewhat portly individual, with a large round face, partly hidden behind small round eyeglasses. He moved with a force and energy that had always impressed Raider, who knew McParland for what he was —one hell of a tough hombre. "Goddamn it, Raider," he snapped. "We've been looking all over hell for you for the past week."

"Well, you found me, and this ain't exactly hell."

"There are those who would disagree," McParland sniffed, looking around disapprovingly at the overlush decor.

Where'd he get so prissy all of a sudden? Raider wondered.

"To finally find you in a whorehouse..." McParland continued.

"Watch your mouth!" Raider and Miss Livonia chorused together again.

McParland controlled himself with obvious difficulty. He had always been a driving sort of man, the kind who had trouble just being somewhere without trying to change it. Maybe, Raider thought, that was why he'd gotten to where he was.

"You're supposed to check in regularly. Keep us informed of your whereabouts."

"I kinda retired for a while."

"Nevertheless."

"Anyhow, you ain't been goin' outta your way to bring me any work."

"Things have been a little slow." A suspicious look came over McParland's big beefy face. "Say, you didn't take any reward money on that last case, did you?"

"Hell no."

"Because you know that operatives aren't supposed to—"

"I just said that I didn't."

McParland gave Raider a long appraising look, then his eyes worked their way around the opulent room, then back to Raider, who was not exactly the picture of prosperity, standing there in his dusty denim trousers and frayed black shirt. "If you didn't get hold of some extra money," he said weightily, "then how the hell can you afford to hang out in an expensive whore... in a place like this?"

Raider smiled. "Ain't expensive at all. They like me here."

"You mean you get it for free?" McParland asked disbelievingly. "I've heard of the whore with the heart of gold, but I always figured her heart got that way because of all the gold she sucked outta men."

"That kind of talk," Livonia cut in icily, "is not going to make you many friends in this house, mister."

"I think I can live with that," McParland replied just as icily.

The Pinkerton and the madam stood facing one another with obvious hostility. Raider grinned and tried to slip away unnoticed. Maybe while they fought it out—and it ought to be one hell of a battle—he could mosey on upstairs and let Mae show him some of her exercise tricks. But it was not to be. There was a sudden burst of noise from the rear of the house, a woman's scream, a man's snarling voice, and a moment later a naked girl, clutching a scrap of clothing in front of her nubile young body, came running into the parlor, screaming back over her shoulder, "I don't do that kinda thing! You can't make me!"

A huge bearded man, stuffing his shirttail into his pants, came striding along behind the girl. "I paid my money, you bitch," he roared. "And I'll damn sure get my money's worth."

He stopped as he came into the parlor, somewhat surprised to find himself facing so many people. "What might be bothering you, sport?" Livonia asked, interposing her bulk between the man and the cowering, naked girl.

"I paid my money, I didn't get what I wanted," he snarled.

"Maybe what you wanted isn't available here," Livonia said coldly. She reached into some secret recess of her voluminous dress and, pulling out a five-dollar gold piece, tried to hand it to the man.

Raider saw stubbornness settle over the man's rather

brutal features. "Don't want my money back. I want what I come here for. Damned bitch, gettin' a man all heated up, then puttin' on that too-pure-to-do-it act."

"He wanted me to..." the girl started to whimper. Livonia hushed her. The man moved forward, obviously intending to go around Livonia and head for the girl. Raider put his hand on the man's chest and stopped him. "I suggest you take the money and try someplace else," he said quietly.

The man's face slowly faded from bright red to a deeper red, a killing red. "You tryin' to butt in on me, buddy."

"There's a place down by the railroad tracks," Raider continued. "It's for winos, drunks, and perverts. It oughta suit you just fine."

"Why, you son of a bitch."

The man had a pistol stuck into the waistband of his dirty trousers, and now he reached for it. The naked girl screamed, Livonia cursed, and McParland, his hand reaching inside his coat for the small pistol he carried in a shoulder holster, found himself blocked by the madam's vast bulk.

Not that it mattered. Moving with an easy, graceful speed, Raider, unarmed, picked up a heavy brass ashtray from the bar top and threw it backhanded at the gunman. The ashtray bounced off the man's skull with a loud metallic ringing. The man grunted and fell over backward, the gun pointed harmlessly at the ceiling. Raider took it from his hand before he even hit the floor. Laying the pistol on the bar top, careful not to mar the shiny wood—Miss Livonia was touchy about her bar top—Raider reached down, took the man by the back of his collar, dragged him across the floor, out of the parlor, through the front hall, then tossed him down the steps into the dusty street. "Remember," Raider said as the man struggled to sit up. "Down by the railroad tracks. They'll have what you want."

Raider slammed the front door and walked unconcernedly back into the parlor. Livonia had seated the weeping girl on a couch and was comforting her. McParland was looking away, obviously somewhat ill at ease with the girl's nakedness. Livonia turned to face him. "See? That's one of the reasons Raider doesn't need any money in my house. We like having him around."

McParland looked at her icily as she turned back to the girl. Then he stepped close to Raider. "Goddamn if I ain't seen it all now," he said in a low disgusted voice. "One of the agency's finest operatives working as a bouncer in a Texas whorehouse."

Raider's eyes grew just as icy. "I'm gonna go on tryin' to respect you, McParland. But you're gonna have to learn to watch your mouth. Now, get off your preachin' an' tell me why the hell you been lookin' for me."

Being a good judge of men, McParland knew he'd gone just about as far with Raider as a man could safely go. Swallowing an angry retort, he said, "We have an assignment for you. The client asked for you personally."

"Yeah? Who is it?"

"Andrew Onderdonk."

Raider looked puzzled. "Onderdonk? Well, I think I mighta heard the name somewhere, but I can't connect it to a face."

"New Yorker. Big-time builder and engineer. Built the sea wall in San Francisco. He's building a railroad up in British Columbia, which is where the trouble is."

"Still don't know him. Wonder how he got my name."

"Asked especially for you."

Light dawned in Raider's eyes. "Wait. He's a rich Easterner?"

"Yeah. Had money all his life."

Raider nodded. "Gotta be Doc. He likes runnin' around with all them rich bastards. Musta given him my name. He'd do that."

Raider was talking about his former partner and longtime Pinkerton operative, Doc Weatherbee, a Boston man of some breeding, who had married a few years earlier.

"Must be one miserable son of a bitch of a job if Doc's wishin' it on me."

"You know Weatherbee better than that," McParland said testily. "Although I admit that it does sound like a rather difficult assignment. Even though he's an American, Onderdonk won the contract to build the western segment of the new trans-Canadian railroad. He was doing okay until recently, when he started having a lot of labor trouble and accidents. Only he doesn't think they're accidents, he thinks that what's been happening to his project involves deliberate sabotage. He wants the agency to do something about it. We said we'd send a man up there to look into it, make sure he's right, and then recommend what should be done."

"Hell, that should be easy enough. If people are sabotaging the man's railroad, he'll probably want us to just go ahead and sack their saddles, you know ... send 'em on up to Saint Peter for a little harp practice."

"Canada's a separate country, Raider. We can't trample on Canadian law. You'll have to use tact, watch your step.... Oh hell, I'll never understand why Onderdonk specified you."

"Well, I'll do it anyhow. Gettin' a little rusty sittin' around here. Maybe even gettin' fat." He thoughtfully checked the place on his belly where Mae had pinched him.

"Good enough. We'll give you travel money to British Columbia. When can you leave?"

Raider looked up the stairs, toward Mae's room. "In a couple of hours. Gotta do my exercises first."

CHAPTER THREE

As it turned out, Raider did not depart until the next morning. The news of his leaving spread quickly throughout Miss Livonia's establishment. Each of her girls seemed to develop a burning desire to say goodbye to Raider. A personal goodbye. Very personal. By that evening Raider had had all the exercise a man could stand without the danger of suffering serious, long-term damage.

The next morning, Miss Livonia stood on the upstairs terrace, watching as Raider tossed his saddle, bridle, saddlebags, bedroll, and rifle into the buckboard for the short ride to the train station. Female heads were poking out of windows both upstairs and down—blond heads, brunette heads, heads with raven hair. Miss Livonia felt a heavy pang deep inside her massive breast as she watched Raider climb up onto the seat of the buckboard, then stop a moment, grinning up at the windows. A chorus of soft sighs and goodbyes rustled through the building.

Miss Livonia realized that there was nothing phony about this show of emotion, none of it was being put on.

She knew that the girls would genuinely miss Raider. Awash in nostalgia, she remembered how it had been when she'd been a working girl herself—all that daily rabbitstyle sex with so little to it: Miners, cowboys, gamblers, ranchers—quick, unsatisfying bed struggles with strangers, engendering the need for something more satisfying, for someone who would really, but *really* make love to them, someone, a friend if not actually a lover, someone of their own to sate their bodies' normal needs. Uh-huh. The ever-present dream of the working girl, usually unrealized. Miss Livonia gave a sigh of her own. Twenty years ago, when she had not been so damned fat, maybe she too would have spent some time with Raider. But what the hell? So she'd traded the pleasures of the bed for the pleasures of the table. Not a total loss. Not at all.

Raider flicked the reins, and the horses, full of energy this early in the morning, tossed their heads, then threw themselves against the harness, and a moment later the buckboard was clattering down the street. Raider turned for one last wave, then swung his head forward, sawing on the reins. There was one final mass groan from the whorehouse windows, then pretty heads moved back out of sight, their owners mentally preparing for another humdrum night's work.

Raider's reaction was considerably different. Over the past month he'd had one hell of a good time at Livonia's place. Hell, he'd been practically wallowing in women. But for the past couple of weeks, time had begun to drag. His main feeling as he headed for the train station was one of release. Back on the trail again, on the move, adventure ahead, good memories behind. What more could a man ask?

When he reached the station, Raider paid a porter fifty cents to drive the buckboard back to Miss Livonia's, then he put his saddle and other horse gear into the baggage car, but took his bedroll and rifle with him into the passenger car. He didn't like being separated from his weapons. And he could use his bedroll for a pillow during the long trip.

THE NORTHWEST RAILROAD WAR 21

The Pinkerton National Detective Agency did a lot of work for the railroads. Most Pinkerton operatives carried permanent railroad passes. They were only second-class passes, which were a damned sight better than immigrant class, although definitely lacking the luxuries and comfort of first class. Not that Raider minded; luxury had seldom formed much of a part of his life. Born on a hardscrabble Arkansas farm, he'd gotten out while still in his teens. For a couple of years he'd survived by breaking his back for others—until he discovered that his innate skill with weapons, and with his fists and feet, opened a path to another style of living, which, while it might involve considerable physical discomfort and risk, at least saved him from the curse of regular work and regular hours. He was hired by the Pinkerton National Detective Agency. He'd been able to live a life of movement, adventure, and relative freedom, each day bringing something new and challenging, always on the move, mostly across the vastness of the West.

A vastness that was quickly shrinking. A little over a dozen years ago, a trip from Texas to British Columbia would have taken months. And maybe a traveler's life. Now, with railroads running all over the damned place, a man could travel coast to coast in less than a week. Which meant that dirt farmers from the East, people seeking the kind of life Raider had long ago abandoned, would continue pouring into what had, only a few years ago, been virgin land. And here he was, on his way up north to help some Easterner build another goddamned railroad, way up there in Canada, one more frontier shot to hell. Well, you really couldn't fight it.

As the train got under way, Raider settled into his hard wooden seat. A little later he spread out the bedroll to soften the impact of his ass. A couple of hours on these goddamn benches was worse than a week in the saddle.

Only two or three years earlier, to get to the West Coast, Raider would have had to head north, passing through Denver and Cheyenne, to connect with the Central Pacific line, the only east-west rails going all the way through. But now the Southern Pacific had laid down tracks all the way to California, through the Southwest.

The train rattled on, into the flat barrenness of West Texas, hour after hour of changeless desolation. By the time the train reached El Paso, it was night, and Raider was stretched out on his bedroll, asleep. In the morning he woke up to New Mexico, to a more interesting land, more diverse, true desert, with dry eroded hills thrusting up out of the sand and sagebrush. The next day saw the train passing through Arizona, an even more diverse landscape: saguaro cactus, Joshua trees, ocatillo, more moonscape mountains.

That evening the train made a short stop in Tucson. Looking out the train window, bored, Raider saw the same old flat-roofed one-story adobes that had been there the last time he'd passed through, the same wide dusty main street. But he also noticed a number of telephone poles. Another newfangled invention. Yep. A few years more and a man wouldn't be able to escape at all from some other man's endless yapping.

The land began to grow mountainous, more rugged, interesting, pine-clad. Raider wished he were out there riding over the ground on horseback, able to smell the sage, hear the thud of his horse's hooves against the clean sandy soil. That would be a hell of a lot better than sitting here on his ass, smelling the stench of burning coal.

The train passed through the pine-clad highlands near Wickenburg, then descended into the torrid heat near the California border, a foretaste of hell, a country that had killed many a traveler before the arrival of the iron horse.

Raider arrived in Los Angeles the morning of the fourth day. He left the train and took his gear into town, except for the horse furniture, which he left checked at the baggage department. In the morning he'd have to change to a train heading north, but, by God, first he'd get off his ass for a night. He took a room in a small hotel just down the street from the Pico House, the posh kind of place his ex-partner, Doc, had always finagled them into. Raider hated the place. Full of goddamned flunkies who never let you do anything for yourself.

After a wash and a shave, Raider headed out into the streets for some food and drink, and maybe a little fun. He was astounded by the changes in the city. The place was growing like a weed. And why not? He'd seen copies of those fucking advertisements that had been showing up in the eastern papers, touting the chance to buy a small California lot, sight-unseen, and move on out to paradise. Those eastern tenderfeet were flocking out to the Coast like lemmings. Too bad they didn't copy lemmings all the way, and fall right off the edge of the land into the sea.

Raider walked down to Sonoratown, the Mexican part of Los Angeles. He felt more comfortable here, away from the big buildings and the streetcars. He found a little cantina, where he had a meal of tamales and steak, with rice and beans, which he washed down with lots of beer. Gently burping, he headed back toward town, but away from the hotel and into the mean part, The Calle de los Negros, looking for a card room he'd visited a few years before. A game or two of poker before turning in would round the day out real nice.

The card room was still there. Raider wandered in, and a few minutes later had bought his way into a game, using some of his Pinkerton expense money as a stake. He was not a man who lived for gambling, but with his lack of fear and power of concentration, he had usually been able to augment his income at the tables. Not unusual for a western lawman.

After an hour, he was about forty dollars ahead. With his head buried in his cards, he was vaguely aware of someone standing nearby, waiting for a chance to buy into the game. At first he didn't look up when the man finally pulled out a chair, sat down, and said his howdies. Then Raider was immediately aware that he'd heard that voice before. Looking up, he caught the eye of a plumpish, rather garishly dressed little man, wearing a seedy suit and vest, with a dented derby perched rakishly on his round head.

"Well, goddamn my eyes," Raider murmured. "If it ain't Happy Jack O'Reilly."

The little man turned somewhat green when he recognized Raider, but, recovering with admirable speed, he nodded in a friendly enough manner, even managing something approaching a smile. "Glad to see you, Raider. You're looking real fine. Prosperous, too," he added, pointing to the stack of chips in front of the big Pinkerton.

"Let's hope it stays that way," Raider responded with a slight nod. "'Cause if I catch you cheatin', I'll reach right down your throat, grab you by the ass, and turn you inside out."

Happy Jack looked aggrieved. "Now, is that a way to talk to an old friend?"

Raider grunted, then returned to his cards. Happy Jack O'Reilly was not exactly an old friend. Raider knew him as a small-time grifter and confidence man. A few years before he'd helped put him in jail after the agency had caught him out in a land swindle scheme. Raider had kind of hated to do it; he'd had to admit that the men Happy Jack had swindled were the kind who deserved swindling—fat-cat greedy bastards who thought they smelled a killing, who had actually thought they were swindling Happy Jack. But the law was the law, and those men had the clout, and Happy Jack went into the jug. He'd never seemed to bear Raider any grudge. His arrest, trial, and sentence were merely part of the cost of doing his particular kind of business. He was essentially a happy-go-lucky, harmless little bastard—unless you had some money in your pocket and didn't know how to hang on to it.

Tonight, Happy Jack seemed to be going out of his way to be nice to Raider. Although he won a fair amount of money, he made sure that Raider won too. Raider had never seen a man handle the pasteboards like Happy Jack. He knew the little grifter was probably cheating, but damned if he could tell how. If Happy Jack hadn't been so goddamned lazy, he might have been a rich man by now, but he seemed to be able to piss away his money as quickly as he earned it.

Raider left the card room over sixty dollars ahead. On his way back to his hotel, he passed a whorehouse, but was not particularly tempted. The passionate goodbyes at Miss Livonia's were probably going to last him for quite a while.

The next morning he was on the first train heading north. He thought he saw Happy Jack getting into the first-class car, but was not sure. Well, what the hell. What did it matter, anyhow? It was a free country.

It was a day and a half run up to San Francisco, so Raider settled back in his seat as the train headed over the Los Angeles plain, then up into the rugged mountains a few miles to the north. A little while later daylight was snuffed out as the train headed into the first of the tunnels. All through the day the scenery alternated between mountains and rich valleys. Night came on, the miles clicked away, and the next morning the train arrived in Sacramento, where Raider changed to a train that took him to the eastern side of San Francisco Bay. He hired a man to help him carry his gear to the ferry, and a short while later was standing on the ferryboat's big flat deck, with the low Berkeley Hills at his back. San Francisco lay straight ahead, a low sprawl of buildings undulating over the city's many hills.

San Francisco was one of the few cities Raider could stomach. There was an infectious air of enthusiasm about it, and it was such a damned pretty place. You could see the deep blue of the bay from so many viewpoints. The inhabitants had an easy manner, a sense of liveliness.

After checking into a hotel, he bought a horse. He'd been warned that, because of the railroad building boom, horses were expensive in British Columbia. He bought the big bay that looked like it had both staying power and intelligence. Raider knew that stupid horses had killed more men than gunfire. Of course, he also realized that an intelligent horse would always try to take a chunk out of your hide if you got careless; they were too smart to think much of the idea of a human climbing onto their back. But Raider never had trouble teaching a horse who was boss. He had no romantic notions about horses. They were transportation. If you took good care of a horse, it'd get you where you were going. If it crapped out, you could always get another one.

Raider stayed in San Francisco two days, much of his time spent riding the cable cars up and down the hills, the rest of the time spent eating. San Francisco had more restaurants per capita than any other city in the country. Good ones, too, so he made the most of the opportunity.

From San Francisco he would travel to British Columbia by ship. The overland route to Canada was a difficult one. Damned beautiful, too, but Andrew Onderdonk wasn't going to wait around forever for him to show up. So, early one morning, he boarded a steamship that would stop at Seattle, Victoria, and, finally, New Westminster in British Columbia. It was a typical foggy San Francisco morning, but by the time the ship had gotten under way and was about to pass through the Golden Gate, the fog lifted. The sun's rays struck through the thinning fog, lighting up the city bit by bit. Goddamn nice—for a city.

Raider stood at the rail until the sheer cliffs of the Golden Gate shut out the view, then he made his way toward the salon, hoping to find something to eat. He spotted a lunch counter and headed toward it, noticing that some eager punters had already started a poker game at a table in the center of the salon. He might have walked on by, but once again a familiar voice intruded into his consciousness. Raider turned quickly, his eyes searching out the familiar, round little figure.

Yep, there he was. Happy Jack O'Reilly, raking in a pot.

CHAPTER FOUR

Happy Jack, absorbed in his cards, did not see Raider. Raider kept his back to the card table, bought his breakfast, and took it out onto the deck. While he ate, he watched the land slide by. After an hour or two the boat had moved too far out to sea for him to make out much detail. He was preparing to go back to his cabin when he saw Happy Jack come out onto the deck, smiling and patting his pocket. Obviously the game had been profitable.

Raider moved in behind Happy Jack. "I'd hate to think you'd been followin' me," he growled into the little man's ear. Happy Jack literally leaped into the air, then spun around to face Raider, his jaw working soundlessly. The instinctive look of fear and surprise on the little gambler's face suggested to Raider that maybe Happy Jack was sure *he* was the one being followed. "Following you? Oh, no. Nothing of the sort," he burst out. "I had no idea at all that you were on this boat."

"Yeah? Well, I wish the hell *you* weren't on it. Where you headin'?"

"As far as the boat goes. British Columbia."

"The *hell* you say! Well, you listen to me. It would make me a whole lot happier if you got off, say, in Seattle. Sound good to you?"

"Oh, no. I couldn't do that," Happy Jack said, shaking his head vehemently. "I got my passage paid for all the way through to British Columbia, and that's where I intend to go."

"And if I say different?"

"It won't make me change my mind," the little man said stubbornly. "This is a free country, and I can go where I like. Besides," he said, a slight note of pleading entering his voice, "with all the railroad building going on up there, all the payrolls, think of the men who are going to want to play cards! I need the money, Raider. Buying this boat ticket took my last cent. It's make or break, and British Columbia could be the making of me. I *have* to go."

Happy Jack was leaking the spirit of American free enterprise all over the deck. Raider figured it was just as likely someone was looking for the little swindler somewhere back in the States, and Happy Jack had figured it was time to make tracks. Not that Raider was going to do much about it anyhow. He kind of liked the little grifter, although having him here could be a problem. "Just one thing," Raider growled. "When we get up to British Columbia, you make sure that you don't know me from Adam. Okay? You don't know who I am or what I do."

Happy Jack's face lit up. "You're on a case, right?"

"Maybe. Just remember what I said. You don't know me."

Happy Jack nodded enthusiastically. "Okay, Raider, anything you say. But if you need any help..."

Raider groaned silently. It was truly amazing how many people were thrilled with the idea of working with the dreaded Pinkertons. Even men the agency had helped put into the slammer. That's all it would take to foul up this operation—an amateur getting in the way.

"Just butt out, O'Reilly. You don't know me, you never seen me before."

"Sure, sure, I understand."

Raider walked away, muttering under his breath. Fortunately he only saw Happy Jack a couple of more times during the voyage. Each time Happy Jack studiously avoided meeting Raider's eye—until, when he believed no one else was looking, he'd slip Raider a huge wink. Which did little to improve the Pinkerton's mood.

Near the end of the third day out, the boat passed Humboldt Bay, but quite a ways out from the shore, so that all Raider could see of the area was the huge cloud of smoke and dirt that hung over the land, thanks to the lumber mills that dominated the area. More than once, Pinkerton business had taken Raider to the Humboldt Bay region. They'd been difficult cases, and the land hadn't helped. It was hard land, a real wilderness, nothing but mountains and forests for as far as the eye could see. He expected pretty much the same thing when he reached British Columbia. But colder.

A couple of days later the boat stopped in Seattle. Raider remained aboard. He noticed that Happy Jack did too, which reinforced his opinion that maybe Happy Jack was worried about somebody looking for him. Part of the wages of sin.

They were under way again the next day. This was the shortest leg of the trip, up through the San Juan Islands, heading for the mouth of the Fraser River.

As he usually did before starting out on a case, Raider had tried to learn all he could about the area where he would be operating. Not that there was a whole lot to learn about British Columbia. It was still more or less empty, practically uninhabited. The Spanish had taken a short look a few hundred years earlier, claiming it for Spain, of course, as they always did with any chunk of land or body of water they might pass near. Later, the Englishman Captain George Vancouver had charted and mapped what was now Vancouver Island, plus parts of the mainland. British

Columbia had become a British Crown Colony only a couple of decades earlier, when the English had become nervous about Russian encroachments on the northwest coast. But for a long time, the only white men in the area were fur trappers, usually under the aegis of the Hudson's Bay Company. Later, when British Columbia had finally become a part of the new Canadian Union, a lumber boom had sprung up, and now there were a number of busy but small settlements full of loggers, mill workers, and shipping agents. British Columbian lumber, plus British Columbian coal from Vancouver Island, was being shipped to the Orient, to South America, and to San Francisco. And now, with the new railroad nearing completion—if something could be done about the sabotage—British Columbia might be about to get some regular dirt-farmer settlers.

The boat carefully picked its way through the Georgia Straits. Fortunately, it was a beautiful day, with a hard blue sky and good visibility. Heavily wooded rocky islands, some of them fairly large, thrust up haphazardly from the placid, milky blue water. Eventually the mainland loomed ahead, an unbroken wall of forest, except for the broad mouth of the Fraser River estuary, pumping out fresh water into the sea. The boat steamed into the river mouth, and half an hour later it was being tied up at the docks at New Westminster, which was the only sizable town on the coast, with perhaps four thousand regular inhabitants, in addition to the hundreds who passed through on their way into or out of the interior.

New Westminster wasn't much of a town, just a collection of clapboard buildings with an occasional attempt at something more sturdy. Ragged pine and spruce forest ringed the edge of the settled area, with trees and scrub coming right down to the edges of the most recently cleared streets and building lots. The forest, dark and unbroken, stretched inland as far as the eye could see.

Raider supervised the unloading of his horse, glad to see that the animal had made the journey in good shape. He stabled it at a livery not far from the docks, along with his saddle gear, then strode on into town. An hour's dickering, plus some money, gained him a ticket on the paddle-wheel river steamer that would take him upriver, toward the railhead at Fort Yale. He found it a little odd that the coastal portion of the railroad would be the last portion built. So far the only way to get to Fort Yale was by boat or overland, and the overland route was very difficult.

Raider took a room, stowed his gear, then roamed the streets. There was not much to see, just the usual raw frontier town, oversupplied with saloons and gambling halls, which, of course, were packed. The streets were a lot muddier than the streets in most of the American frontier. He'd heard that it rained a lot in these parts, and sure enough, by evening it was raining, a soft but steady drizzle that turned most of the greens to grays. Bored, Raider hit the sack early and was up before dawn, gathering his gear for the trip upriver.

The river steamer was a good-sized stern-wheeler, although lacking the luxurious appointments of the Mississippi steamboats. This was a no-nonsense craft for hauling goods and men upriver, to where the work was. Raider made sure his horse was loaded aboard properly, then found a place to sit. He saw Happy Jack come aboard, but turned away before the little bastard could wink.

The boat's big steam engines began to chuff mightily. Clouds of steam disappeared up into a low morning overcast. Lines were cast off, and in a few minutes they were under way, chugging up the broad expanse of the lower Fraser. Within a short while New Westminster, the last connection with the outside world, had disappeared behind them.

Once away from the coast, the clouds disappeared and a warm sun beat down upon the land. The farther upstream they went, the more the river narrowed. The shores were relatively devoid of any evidence of human habitation. Heavy forest came right down to the water. Away from the river the land rose steeply, undulating away in range after range of tremendously rugged mountains. It was a new place, Raider thought. Hardly used yet. That wouldn't last for long. The trees would go first, the virgin stands of timber, being replaced eventually by scrubby second growth. The flatter areas would be scraped clean by dirt-grubbing farmers, with their scrawny wives and snot-nosed brats. The Indians would either start working for the white men or get steamrollered. Yep. Civilization would fix the place up real fast.

Eventually the river became even narrower. At Harrison the passengers and cargo were transferred to a smaller vessel. The trip became much rougher, with the little steamer occasionally battling rapids. They finally made Yale just as it was getting dark; night fell at about ten o'clock this time of year. Raider collected his horse, saw that it was adequately boarded at a livery stable, then checked into a local hotel. It was actually more a workman's rooming house than a hotel, a big bare place in which Raider was lucky to get a room to himself. A few minutes later he was out on the street, looking for the man he was supposed to meet, Michael Haney.

As he'd been told to do, he went first to the railroad construction offices. Surprisingly, they were open. Raider told a clerk who he was looking for. Ten minutes later Haney came into the office, looking slightly unsteady on his feet, as if he'd been drinking. When he spoke, his breath confirmed it. "Thought you'd never get here," Haney said loudly.

"It was a fair piece up the road."

"Yes, yes, of course. Well, let me take you up to meet A.O. He told me to bring you to the house the moment you got in, as long as I could keep anyone else from seeing you. He felt that if it was known you had a connection with us..."

Raider nodded, hoping his terseness would cut off the seemingly endless flow of Haney's chatter. Maybe he just talked like this when he'd had a few. He hoped so.

Haney led the way out of the building. It was dark out now; Raider doubted they'd be noticed. He was of two minds about being connected to the railroad management. On the one hand, anonymity meant that he'd be able to go a lot of places, hear a lot of talk that a known railroad agent couldn't. On the other hand, if it were known that a man was on the job, ready to make it hot for saboteurs, that might help too.

When Haney took Raider up onto the big veranda of Onderdonk's house, the front door was open to let in the air, although a screen door kept out the abundant insect life; it was a warm night.

Mrs. Onderdonk looked up, surprised, when Haney knocked, then smiled and came over to unhook the screen door. "Andrew's in his study," she said. "I'll tell him you're here."

Onderdonk must have heard them talking, because he immediately came out to meet them. He noticed Raider, and looked questioningly at Haney. "It's him. He's here," Haney said somewhat theatrically.

Onderdonk nodded, then led the way into the office. Seating himself behind a desk, he motioned the other two men toward chairs. "Do you know why you're here?" he asked Raider.

"Something about sabotage."

Onderdonk nodded again. Raider was happy to see that, unlike Haney, the man didn't waste words. He was impressed with Onderdonk's general demeanor and looks. It helped a lot when you were working for a man who knew how to keep his mouth shut.

"I suppose there's no way to prove that systematic sabotage is going on," Onderdonk said. "But there's no doubt in my mind that that's the case."

"Any idea who's doing it?"

Onderdonk shook his head again.

"Maybe it's one of the contractors that bid for the job and lost it," Haney interjected. Raider looked questioningly at Onderdonk, who merely shrugged. Definitely not a man to waste words.

"How's it happening? What kind of sabotage?"

"Just accidents, mostly," Onderdonk said. "Roadbeds that fall away under wagons. Draft animals that die of mysterious ailments. One time there was an unplanned explosion that we know for a fact was not an accident, because we saw the man who set it off running away from the scene. And lately, trouble with the workers. Especially the coolies."

"Chinese?"

Onderdonk nodded again. Raider waited for him to enlarge on the subject, but it was Haney who spoke. "We have thousands of them here. For a long time there was a terrible manpower shortage. We tried bringing in French-Canadians, but not enough of them came, and they don't really like working for English-speakers anyhow. We tried bringing men up from San Francisco, but the kind of waterfront scum who were willing to come way up here were not worth their wages—drunks and troublemakers. So Mr. Onderdonk brought over shiploads of Chinamen from southern China. That did the trick. They're good workers, and up until now they hadn't given us any trouble."

"How do the locals feel about Chinese labor?"

"Well, that's part of the problem. There's been high feeling against coolie labor from the start. The people here were afraid the Chinese would take away their jobs, work for less."

"What do you pay the Chinese?"

"A dollar a day."

"And the white men?"

"Two dollars."

Haney, uncomfortable under Raider's gaze, although the Pinkerton had said nothing more, tried to justify himself—or Onderdonk. "The Chinese are happy to have the money, and there just weren't enough whites willing to work, anyhow. Besides, that part of it is between the coolies and their agents, the Five Companies. They take care of the coolies' interests. After all, they're Chinese too."

"Yeah. Yeah. I'll bet they're real benevolent people. Well, the Chinese built one hell of a lot of the Central

Pacific, too. I don't remember much trouble from them. What's been happening up here?"

"Someone's been stirring them up. Saying that they're not going to be paid the agreed wages. Saying that the Chinese have to take greater risks than white men. Some of the Chinese work gangs have been refusing to work. One time they attacked a white foreman, nearly killed him. That angered the white workers, and a gang of them attacked a Chinese work gang. Killed two of them. Right now, work has slowed down all along the line."

Raider looked over at Onderdonk. "Anything else?"

Onderdonk shook his head. A real wordy man.

"All right," Raider said, standing up. "I'll start with the Chinese thing, if it feels right."

"Well, how will you be working?" Haney asked.

"Just movin' around. Seein' what I can see."

Onderdonk nodded again, apparently satisfied. Haney still seemed a little confused.

"One more thing," Raider said. "What's the law like around these parts?"

Haney gave a short laugh. "Precious little of it. There are magistrates back at the coast. And we have one Mountie who comes through now and then. One single Mountie, for an area nearly the size of England."

"What kind of man is this Mountie?"

"Well, pretty impressive, I have to admit. His name is Douglas Stuart. Sergeant Douglas Stuart. If we had another dozen like him . . . But there are only three hundred Mounties all together in all of western Canada, spread over an area larger than Europe."

Raider nodded. He'd heard of the Northwest Mounted Police, a paramilitary force that had been formed only a few years earlier. They had a good reputation. But if there was only one man here at this railhead, with all its attendant violence and danger . . .

"Sergeant Stuart may not be terribly happy if he hears you're operating in his area," Haney added somewhat hesitantly. "The local authorities take Canadian sovereignty quite seriously. The lower the profile you maintain, the better."

"Don't worry. I won't shoot anybody out in front of your office," Raider replied laconically. "Now..."

He had turned to leave. Haney stepped forward. "But don't you want us to tell you where the trouble is?"

Raider shrugged, but looked toward Onderdonk, not Haney. "Oh, if there's trouble, I'll find it all right."

CHAPTER FIVE

The next morning Raider began an exploratory swing through the area. There was about a hundred miles to cover. Saddling up his horse and packing his gear, he set out on the old wagon road that had been built to supply the mining camps during the Cariboo gold rush of twenty years earlier.

He'd come close to joining that gold rush himself, but he'd been a rather raw youth at the time, and had gotten himself tied up with an older woman for a few months down in California. She'd taught him tricks he was still wondering about. It had been a rather short gold rush, and by the time he had shaken free of the woman, or rather by the time she had decided it was time for him to move on, the British Columbia gold rush was just about over.

He knew some of its background. During the rush, the interior of British Columbia, until then pretty empty of white men, and not too full of Indians either, had prospered. Firewood and lumber were needed for the wild boomtowns that sprang up practically overnight, so the lumber business prospered. Beef was needed to feed the small army of miners and hangers-on who'd flooded into the area, so ranches were hacked out of the wilderness.

It was the usual cycle of boom then bust. After the gold petered out, the miners departed. With the men gone, the mining towns languished. The budding ranches now had no one to sell their beef to; without a railroad there was really no way to ship it out. The entire province fell on hard times—until the coming of the railroad.

For years the people of British Columbia had been screaming for a railroad, threatening the government in Ottawa with secession unless this isolated province could be connected with the rest of the country. There had even been talk of joining British Columbia to the United States. Hell, a British Columbian could get to San Francisco in a fraction of the time it took him to get to Ottawa or Toronto.

But finally the railroad was becoming a reality, and British Columbia was already prospering. The ranches in the interior now sold their beef to feed the large numbers of men working on the railroad. Loggers and sawmill workers swarmed in to provide the vast amounts of lumber needed to build the seemingly endless bridges and trestles that spanned ravines and rivers so that the rails could maintain a reasonable grade over the rugged landscape. Money was flooding into British Columbia, and Raider knew that wherever there was money, there were bound to be people scheming to get a big chunk of it for themselves. He had little doubt that the sabotage on Onderdonk's road had to do with money, with business—if indeed there really was any sabotage. There was always the possibility that the whole thing was simply an artificial creation within a worried man's overwrought imagination. Not that Onderdonk struck him as a man who saw ghosts.

Raider took his time; there was a lot to see. In many places the old wagon road paralleled the new rails. It wasn't much of a road: it was rough, winding, narrow, and dangerous, subject to landslides, washouts, and general deterioration. He rode along slowly, intent on digesting as much of the scene as he could. The traffic was horrendous; a great deal of the supplies needed by the construction crews still had to travel up the road. Enormous freight wagons followed closely, one behind the other, drawn by big teams of horses and mules. When a wagon reached a narrow spot and met another coming the other way, drivers cursed and swore at one another, each demanding the right of way. Fights often broke out before it was decided who would back up to let the other through.

Raider's respect for Onderdonk's ability as an engineer mounted as he saw the kind of country he'd so far driven the rails through. A lot of the construction was work for hard-rock miners. Tunnel after tunnel had been blasted through adamantine granite.

It was a bridge-builders railroad too. Some of the trestles spanning the riverbeds and canyons were the longest and highest Raider had ever seen. On the second day out, while he sat his horse admiring one enormous span, one of the workmen proudly told him that it contained more than two million board feet of lumber. That was a lot of trees.

The construction zone swarmed with workmen. It wouldn't be easy to pick a few saboteurs out of such a mass of miscellaneous humanity. There were Canadians, both French and English; Métis from the Canadian prairie provinces; Americans from south of the border; Irish; Germans; Indians; and, of course, the Chinese. Thousands of Chinese, living apart in large encampments run by representatives of the Five Companies, the Chinese contractors who had arranged for the coolies' passage to the New World. Each Chinese camp had its own cook and its own liaison with the Anglo world. The coolies dressed, for the most part, in the same garb they had worn in China: baggy pants, loose jackets with high necks, and flat shoes. Most still had their hair hanging down their back in a single pigtail. Few spoke English.

Raider stopped to watch a gallery being blasted out of the side of the mountain. The mountainside was nearly sheer at this point. The plan was to blast out a long section that would be open on one side, like a three-sided tunnel, with rock below, above, and on the side lying against the mountain.

Since the mountainside was not only sheer at this point, but also wet and slippery, there was no possibility of the men climbing it. Instead, men were lowered from above, at the end of long ropes, swinging precariously against the cliff face while they pounded blast holes in the hard rock with a hammer and hand drill.

It was dangerous work. Sometimes a rope broke or slipped, and the man suspended from it fell all the way to the bottom of the cliffs. Occasionally there was a problem with blasting. Each man, working alone on the rock face, had to tamp in his own charge, light the fuse, then give a signal for the men above to haul him up before the charge exploded. Sometimes the charge went off prematurely, or those above did not hear, or did not haul fast enough, and the man was blasted right off the face of the mountain.

"The Injuns work best on those cliffs," one grizzled powder monkey told Raider. "Red bastards don't seem to be 'feard o' nothin'. They go down them ropes just to blast out footholds for other men who're gonna do the heavy blastin'. Trouble is, they get paid extra for it, an' when they git a few dollars ahead, they take off to spend it on a big drunk, an' we don't see 'em agin fer days."

A number of times Raider had to seek shelter while blasting proceeded. Once, above Boston Bar, he heard the cry, "Fire in the hole!" barely in time to race his horse into cover behind some boulders. It must have been a particularly long fuse, because the explosion was long in coming. Raider noticed a man standing behind the cover of a tree about two hundred yards from the tunnel mouth where the charge had been set. Impatient because of the delay, the man, a big florid-faced Irishman, poked his nose out from behind the tree so that he could take a look . . . just as the charge went off. Smoke, flame, and debris erupted from the tunnel mouth. Raider was watching as a whirling stone splinter neatly sliced off most of the man's nose.

It was all dangerous work. Injury and death were common. The constant presence of danger and accident was a perfect cover for masking deliberate sabotage. Also, construction was strung out over a hundred miles, and there was as yet no telegraph line between headquarters at Fort Yale and the railhead. The only way to get word to Raider if there was trouble on the line would be by running a special train up the track.

Which was exactly what happened on Raider's third day out. Raider, using a plan he had rigged up with Michael Haney, had been checking in daily by sending messages back to Fort Yale via a trusted train crew member. So Haney knew where Raider was likely to be on that third day. Haney himself came in person on a fast train consisting of just a tender, an engine, and a flatcar. He was lucky to find Raider still there; Raider had been ready to set out on a trail that led deeper into the interior, but had not yet departed. "Hey! Hey, Raider," the big Irishman shouted. "We got trouble."

Raider was surprised that Haney was so openly breaking his cover, although there really was no longer that much cover. Raider had been asking too many people too many questions. And there was no mistaking him for one of the workmen. Not with that big bay horse, the well-worn .44 strapped low on his hip, the huge bowie knife riding high at his belt, and the big Winchester rifle in its saddle scabbard under his left leg. Any man with eyes and a little experience would be able to peg Raider as a gunfighter.

As soon as he'd spotted Raider, Haney had jumped down from the locomotive cab and ran toward him. It would have been a lot more sensible for Raider to ride over toward Haney, but Haney was too excited to wait. "Trouble back up the line," Haney said, panting.

Raider pulled his mount up next to Haney. "What kind of trouble?"

"Two men. Grabbed a loaded freight wagon. Hit the driver over the head, unhitched the horses, then rolled the wagon down a steep grade right into a whole line of wagons. Two men hurt, several horses killed, some wagons wrecked."

"And the men who did it?"

"They rode off. Got clean away."

Raider seemed unperturbed. "Well, we'll see about that."

"You think there's a chance..."

"Don't know yet. Let's head back to where it happened."

Raider had the train back down a ways, until the flatcar was only a couple of yards from a low bank that was about the same height as the flatcar. He urged his horse close to the edge of the bank and let it take a good look at the distance between the bed of the flatcar and the bank. Then he rode back about fifty yards, turned his horse, kicked it into a trot, then a canter, and jumped it from the bank to the flatcar.

By then Haney was back in the engine, giving the engineer his orders. Raider dismounted and held his horse's reins, steadying the animal as the train lurched into motion. The train was soon speeding back down the track, traveling in reverse, the flatcar leading, the engine pushing. Raider spent most of the trip speaking quietly to his horse, gentling the animal, soothing its nervousness.

They reached the site of the accident in less than half an hour. Raider jumped his horse down from the car; the animal was happy to feel solid ground beneath its feet again. Raider tied the reins to a tree, then went over to examine the wreckage.

At this point the old wagon road took a fairly steep drop down a hillside, finally leveling out near a streambed. Raider could see the point, higher up, where the hijacked wagon had been let loose to roll down the slope. At the time it had happened, four loaded freight wagons had been toiling up the slope. The runaway wagon had been very heavy, loaded with stones for roadbed ballast. It had smashed into the side of the leading uphill wagon, sending it over a bank into the stream, then plowed through the team of mules pulling the second wagon, killing several, then swerved again, crashing into the side of the third wagon. Many of the animals hauling the wagons had been killed or injured during the initial impact. The others had panicked, which helped add to the total destruction as the maddened animals raced out of control, pulling their loads off the roadbed and into the stream.

The injured horses had long since been shot. Their bodies, already bloating in the hot sun, were being hauled from the right-of-way by teams of mules. "The injured men?" Raider asked Haney.

"Already on their way back to the infirmary by train. One had a broken leg, there were some cuts and bruises, and the driver of the hijacked rig had one hell of a lump on his head."

"You're sure he didn't just lose control of his wagon and then make up a story?"

Several other men had been standing around, surveying the wrecked wagons. "No way," one cut in. He was a typical muleskinner, big, rugged with a mouth that could peel the hide off an elephant. "I saw some of it. Well, anyhow, I saw the wagon stopped up at the top of the slope. At the time I figured it was Pete Johnson's wagon, but couldn't see nothin' of Pete. Just two sons-a-bitches fiddling with the mules. Seemed to be unhitchin' 'em, an' I was wonderin' if they was thinkin' of hitchin' 'em up some other ways an' maybe backin' the whole shebang down the slope. Then I saw one o' those bastards slip the brake an' jump down from the seat, an' then the wagon started rollin, right down toward us. Well, I'll tell ya, when that wagon hit, I took a flyin' leap off my load. I figure that's the on'y thing saved my lily white ass."

"And the two men?" Raider asked.

"Well, by the time I'd stopped rollin' around on the ground and had a chance to look up, they was hightailin' it outta there like their balls was on fire. Had a coupla horses stashed in the trees. Disappeared up that way." The mule skinner pointed toward the mouth of a small canyon.

Raider nodded, then turned back to Haney. "Did the hijacked driver say anything?"

"Just that two men rode out of the trees straight at him. One of them threw down on him with a pistol, while the other jumped up onto the wagon and cold-cocked him, maybe with another gun. He doesn't remember anything else until he woke up lying in the road, with his head hurting like hell, an' one hell of a lot of yelling and noise coming from down here."

Raider nodded again, then started walking back toward his horse.

"Where are you going?" Haney asked.

Raider stopped and turned back to face him. "Well, where else? To catch me a couple of saboteurs."

CHAPTER SIX

The ground inside the canyon was rocky and sandy, not the best for tracking, not the kind of loamy soil that took a good imprint. Most men would soon have lost the trail of the two saboteurs, but Raider was not an ordinary tracker. Not after all those years of working with, and then later against, the Indians.

For the first few hundred yards tracking was no challenge at all: there was really no other direction the two men could have gone except straight up that narrow canyon. The canyon walls rose nearly sheer. It was not for another half mile that other alternatives offered themselves.

Raider nearly missed the point where the tracks turned off into a bigger canyon. The ground was quite hard here, and if Raider had been unlucky he might have lost half an hour or more, casting around for sign. But the men had been forced by the nature of the terrain to push their mounts through thick brush, causing some damage. It was the fresh gleam of reddish flesh on the inside of broken limbs that alerted Raider.

Up inside this larger canyon, the ground alternated between softer areas, more able to take an imprint, which meant easier tracking, and blank hardpan, which sometimes left Raider wondering. Numerous smaller canyons opened off the larger one. He had to take his time at each potential branching to make sure that his quarry had not cut off to the side.

The day wore on. Raider began to worry about falling too far behind. If the men he was following made it back to the road before he caught up to them, or to Fort Yale, he would quickly lose their tracks among the thousands of hoof- and footprints left by the construction crews and their animals.

He'd been on their trail for about two hours when he found the place where they'd stopped. The terrain was less brushy here; large trees were scattered down the slopes into the floor of the canyon. The men had tied their horses to bushes; he could see where the animals had cropped the grass under the bushes. He could also see where the men had peed against a tree. An area of crushed grass indicated where they'd sat to rest. Most interesting of all, he could see the empty whiskey bottle they'd left behind. Cocky bastards. Obviously they'd figured no one would follow them. A bad mistake.

Raider pushed on. The men seemed to be riding erratically. Their trail meandered all over the canyon floor. He hoped they were as drunk as they seemed. Farther along, he found a second empty bottle glistening from amongst some thick grass alongside the trail. Stupid idiots. He had them now.

Raider came in sight of his quarry about an hour later: two men, slumped in their saddles, riding slowly. In the clear mountain air he could hear them singing drunkenly.

Raider stopped his horse in thick cover. He studied the mountains around him. As far as he could see, this canyon continued on for several more miles. He became interested in a smaller canyon off to the right. He suspected that it led back down to the rail line, probably not too far from Fort

THE NORTHWEST RAILROAD WAR 47

Yale. He decided to drive the men out of the main canyon and into the smaller one.

Riding around to the left, careful to stay out of sight, Raider flanked the two men, traveling in a big circle that put the men between himself and the canyon he wanted to drive them into. When he was in position, he rode out into the open. The two men had stopped about five hundred yards away. They were slapping one another on the back and laughing. Probably telling each other dirty stories.

Raider began to ride slowly toward them, whistling a little tune. He was only four hundred yards away when one of them either heard or saw him coming. Raider saw the man stiffen in his saddle, then furiously poke the other man's upper arm.

To leave no doubt as to why he was there, Raider slipped his rifle from its saddle scabbard and levered a shell into the chamber. The two men immediately reached for their own rifles. Being quite drunk, their motions were slow and clumsy, but Raider suspected they would sober up quickly enough. One man brought his rifle to his shoulder, hesitated, then fired, but the range was four hundred yards, and the bullet flew nearly a yard to Raider's right. He could tell from the sound of the shot that the man was using a Winchester '73. Good. Just as he'd figured.

The other man fumbled with the action of his rifle and finally got off a shot. From the sound of it, another '73. Like the first shot, this one also went wide.

Raider flipped up the leaf sight on his own rifle, moved the crossbar up to the four-hundred-yard mark, then slid off his horse, so that he could rest the forearm of his rifle on the saddle. After a second's relaxed aiming, he fired. The hollow booming roar of his rifle sounded very loud after the lighter bark of the two '73s. Half a second later the hat flew off the head of the first man who'd fired. The man clapped his hand to his head, yelling loudly in fear.

Raider worked the lever of his rifle, feeding another shell into the chamber. This time when he fired, no hats flew off, but the bullet smashed into a rock only a foot to the side of the second man's face. He saw the man flinch away from the flying stone splinters, heard him curse, then the faint yell came back, "Let's get the fuck outta here!"

The two men spun their horses around, one man hauling so hard on the reins that his horse nearly fell, then they were racing away—heading exactly where Raider wanted them to be heading, into the smaller canyon that he hoped led back toward the railroad and Fort Yale.

For the next hour, Raider drove the two men ahead of him. Once they tried to make a stand, to drive him off, but they couldn't. Raider laid enough close shots around them to force them back down the trail again, riding hell for leather.

Raider's advantage lay in his rifle, a Winchester Centennial Model, chambered for the big Winchester .45-75 cartridge. It hit hard and it hit far, throwing a massive 350-grain bullet with incredible accuracy and range, almost as impressively as the big Sharps buffalo guns. The other men's rifles, older Winchester '73 models, fired what were essentially pistol rounds. All Raider had to do was keep his distance and the men would either have to keep running or get shot to pieces.

Raider could, of course, have blasted them out of their saddles with his first shots. But he wanted them alive, wanted to run them to the point where they would be grateful to surrender. Then, maybe, if they were sufficiently demoralized, he could find out who they worked for.

Unfortunately, the two men were more familiar with the area than he was, and by the time he had run them to the point of exhaustion, they were out of the canyon, with Fort Yale only about a mile ahead. Already he could see people on the road below, craning their necks to see what all the shooting was about. Raider had counted on questioning the men in private. He had little doubt that he would have been able to find ways to "persuade" them to give him the information he was after, but now there would be no chance. Once they were among people . . .

Raider raised his rifle again, fired once, then again, one

bullet each for the men's mounts. The horses dropped as if they'd been poleaxed, dumping their riders hard into the dirt. Raider rode up fast. The men had been stunned by the fall, and by the time they regained their wits, Raider was looming above them, his rifle in its scabbard again, his big Remington .44 in his right hand. "On your feet, gents," he said. His voice was quiet but his tone unmistakable. Having seen what Raider could do with a rifle, the men were not about to challenge his skill with a pistol.

"Take off your gunbelts," Raider ordered. "Drop 'em in the dirt."

The men carefully unbuckled their gunbelts and let them fall onto the ground. Raider ordered both of them to move several yards away. "Now your shirts. Take 'em off."

"Huh?" one of the men blurted.

"You deaf? I said take off your shirts."

Grumbling a bit, the men shucked out of their rather ragged shirts, while looking back over their shoulders at the people. There was a little group of workmen standing about a hundred yards away. Some of them were starting to walk toward Raider and the two saboteurs.

"Now your pants and boots. Get 'em off."

"Whaaaat?" the bolder of the two men demanded. "Look, hombre, I don't know what the fuck you think you're doin', but—"

Raider cocked his pistol. The man flinched when he heard the wicked *snick* of the hammer ratcheting back. He looked back at the workmen, who were only about fifty yards away now. Gaining confidence from their proximity, the man leered up at Raider. "You can go to hell, you son of a bitch. I ain't gonna—"

Raider fired. The big .44 slug hit the man's boot heel, very, very close to his foot, knocking his right leg out from beneath him. He went down hard. By the time he had recovered his senses enough to look up, Raider was cocking his pistol again. "The next time I shoot," Raider said quietly, "I'm gonna see how close I can come to your balls without actually hittin' 'em. I hope I'm as good a shot as I think I am. I bet you do too."

The man, white as a sheet, quickly sat up and began pulling off his boots. The other man immediately sat down and proceeded to do the same.

The onlookers had stopped their cautious advance when Raider fired. Now the boldest among them continued on. Raider could see that several had pistols, and they were looking at him suspiciously. "What's goin' on here?" a big man with a thick dark beard demanded.

"Caught me a coupla saboteurs," Raider said. "These are the two men who wrecked all those wagons farther on up the track."

There was a murmur from the workmen. Obviously the news had spread fast, because several of the men began to discuss the wagon wreck—heatedly. A number of them were glaring at the two prisoners, who were now shucking off their pants under the threatening muzzle of Raider's .44.

"Goddamn it!" one man shouted. "They oughta swing! Hell, I coulda been drivin' one of them wagons myself, I coulda got all busted up. Bastards like that..."

There were shouts of agreement from among the workmen. The two saboteurs were now beginning to look very worried. "Hang 'em!" several men shouted.

"Well now, boys," Raider said matter-of-factly. "I don't figure we should go ahead and do that. This here is Canada. I hear they don't much go for lynchin' up this way."

From their speech, most of the men seemed to be Americans, probably up from San Francisco. "Well, what the hell we gonna do with 'em, then?" one man growled.

Raider shrugged. "Guess there ain't much we can do except let 'em go."

Several of the workmen protested angrily. Raider saw that one of them had a big bullwhip coiled over one shoulder, a mule skinner's tool. Raider holstered his pistol. "Lend me your whip," he said to the mule skinner.

The man hesitated a moment, then understood. Smiling,

THE NORTHWEST RAILROAD WAR 51

he tossed the whip up to Raider. Raider turned to the two saboteurs, both of whom were totally naked by now, cowering on the ground, their hands over their crotches. "On your feet," Raider snapped.

They hesitated. Raider flicked the whip out to its full length, then brought his arm forward. The whip's leather poppers exploded against the dirt between the two men. The sharp crack of tortured leather seemed more threatening than the blast of a pistol.

The two men leaped to their feet. "Pick up your pants," Raider ordered. Both men grabbed for their trousers. One of the men tried to scoop up his boots, too, but Raider used the whip again, the slender tip cutting one boot nearly in two. The man dropped both boots as if they were red-hot.

"Now head toward town."

The two naked men began shambling toward Fort Yale. They were horsemen, unused to walking. Their tender feet, accustomed to boots, found the stony ground very hard going. Within fifty yards, both were limping badly. Raider kept them moving, snapping the whip around their heels. Once, when they lagged badly, he laid the whip across their naked backs. The men yelped, danced wildly from the pain for a few seconds, then began to walk much more quickly.

A jeering, laughing group of men surrounded them, some throwing small stones and pieces of wood. The saboteurs hopped along, their feet torn and bleeding. And now a new torment appeared. Attracted by all that bare flesh, clouds of mosquitoes, the perennial blood-hungry curse of the north country, formed around the two men. Welts began to rise, no matter how much they slapped their skin and waved their arms.

Raider marched them straight through town. There were, of course, women in Fort Yale, which added to the men's shame as they were driven naked along the streets. Raider drove them on toward the river dock. He was familiar enough with the boat schedules by now to know that a boat was due to leave downriver within the next half hour.

He herded the men right up the gangplank, still naked. Once aboard, the two men turned to face him.

"Get the hell out of British Columbia," Raider said, his voice deadly. "An' keep right on movin'. 'Cause if I see either of you mangy varmints back this way, you're gonna be wolf-bait."

By now the two men were quickly pulling on their trousers. The mixture of fear, hatred, and relief on their faces suggested to Raider that they wouldn't be likely to return. A shame, in a way, because he would have liked to have questioned them. On the other hand, the example of what had happened to the two men on the boat might give any other potential saboteurs a clear, sharp lesson of what lay in store for them. Maybe enough of a lesson to make them think twice.

Raider turned his horse away and was about to ride up into town when he sensed a nervous stirring in the crowd. He caught sight of a man walking down toward the docks, a flash of a red coat. "Damn," he heard one of the workmen say. "It's that fucking Mountie. Now we're gonna see fur fly."

CHAPTER SEVEN

The Mountie was a perfect picture of imperial British splendor. He wore a scarlet coat with gold fittings. Yellow sergeant's stripes shone brightly against the scarlet sleeves. A white solar topee rose high above the Mountie's brow, shading his tanned face. Everything about him glittered. He strode straight down onto the wharf, eyes front and center, arms swinging in a steady military cadence. The crowd parted before him like the Red Sea parting before Moses.

He walked straight up to Raider, then came to a rather abrupt stop, assuming a more or less parade-rest position, feet spread about shoulder width, his hands clasped tightly behind his back. He was a big man, as big as Raider, and the Pinkerton found himself looking directly across into the Mountie's eyes. They were rather narrow eyes, of a piercing gray color. Stern eyes. The Mountie's mouth was a tight slash of disapproval.

"And what, may I ask," he said to Raider, "was all that about."

Raider looked straight back into those cool gray eyes. One tough hombre. "Those boys busted up some wagons a ways up the road. Hurt some men, did a lot of damage. Some of the workmen were a little riled up about it. So our naked friends started thinkin' about other parts o' the world they might like to visit."

The Mountie continued to stare into Raider's eyes. "Are you generally in the habit of taking the law into your own hands?" he finally asked.

"At the time, there didn't seem to be any law around. I did what I thought I had to do."

The Mountie's eyes narrowed even further. "There's law here now. Canadian law."

He looked past Raider at the boat. It had already slipped its moorings and was chugging out into the river. "If those men have committed a crime here in British Columbia," he said icily, "then they belong to me. They would have been tried in a legal court of law, and if convicted, punished."

"Well, I don't think it would have worked out that way. When they wrecked the wagons, they were too far away for anybody to see their faces. In a court of law any weasel-smart lawyer woulda got 'em off with no trouble at all. This way—"

"Your way," the Mountie said quietly. "Your way is the vigilante way. We do not have vigilantes in Canada. You're welcome to keep vigilantism in San Francisco and Montana, where it belongs. It will not be tolerated here. In British Columbia, it will be the Queen's officers, and only the Queen's officers, who will decide what paths apprehension and punishment will take . . . under the law. Is that clear?"

Those cool gray eyes continued to bore into Raider's. He was tempted to ask where Canadian law had been while the railroad line was being sabotaged, but decided that he would let that wait until a more propitious time. Yeah, until he knew the local legal system a little better, he'd just keep his mouth shut. One wrong word, and this tin-soldier Mountie might just toss him out of the country, which would pretty much put an end to the job he was trying to do. "That's clear, Sarge," he replied evenly. "Next time I find some hombres bustin' up Canada, I'll send you a letter."

There was a slight flicker, perhaps of anger, deep down in those gray eyes, and a moment later the Mountie had spun around on his heels and was marching back up the dock, the heels of his brightly polished boots drumming hard against the wood. Raider studied the knife-edge creases in the back of the man's neatly bloused trousers. "That man's so tight-assed I'll bet he shits steel plate," he muttered acidly.

The crowd was now breaking up. A few minutes before, Raider had been a local hero. Now his presence seemed to make the others nervous. All because of that damned tin-soldier Mountie. Who the hell was he, anyhow?

Raider noticed a burly figure walking rapidly down the slope toward the dock. It was Michael Haney. He walked straight up to Raider. "Mr. Onderdonk heard what happened," Haney said. "He'd like to see you up at the house."

Raider nodded. Collecting his horse, he led it by the reins while he walked along beside Haney.

"Well, I suppose that ends any chance of secrecy," Haney said.

"Yep. Bound to happen sooner or later in a place as cut off as this."

"Mr. Onderdonk is very pleased about you catching those men."

"He seems to be about the only one," Raider muttered irritably, remembering the way that holier-than-thou Mountie had looked at him. Like something that had crawled out from under a rock.

They reached the house without any further conversation. Raider, along with Haney, was ushered into Onderdonk's study. "Capital work, Raider. Too bad you couldn't have hung them."

"Guess that's not permitted around here."

Onderdonk looked puzzled. Haney quickly cut into the conversation. "Raider just met Sergeant Stuart. Stuart came along just after Raider had sent the two men off on the packet boat. Sergeant Stuart was not . . . pleased."

Raider snorted. "That man acts like he eats alum three times a day. Real puckered-up type. What the hell's botherin' him, anyhow?"

Onderdonk shrugged. "History, I suppose. Canada is a new country. It has a lot of land. Rough land, empty land, and without much population to fill it up. From the very beginning, the United States has been, sometimes unwittingly, sometimes with full consciousness, putting pressure on Canada."

"Yeah. That's true," Raider said. "We always did want their land."

"It's been particularly bad out here in the Canadian West. Until only a few years ago, this was just an isolated British Crown Colony. It had no real connection to the rest of Canada at all. It was mainly the preserve of the Hudson's Bay Company. They were Britain's representatives here, and they just barely managed to hold on. Americans were moving in all the time. Old John Jacob Astor, for instance, muscled in on their fur trade and tried to take the whole shebang away."

"A real pirate, old Astor."

Raider waited to see how Onderdonk would react to that. John Jacob Astor was an eastern fat cat. Came from the same strata of society as Onderdonk did. But Onderdonk merely nodded, and then Raider remembered that Astor had fought his way up from nothing. To a man of Onderdonk's privileged birth, Astor probably was just another pirate.

"The Hudson's Bay Company used to have their headquarters down at the mouth of the Columbia River," Onderdonk continued. "The U.S. finished them off there when it forced the British to cede the entire Oregon Territory to the U.S. That didn't sit too well with the Canadians. Of course, there were too few of them to fight us; it was right after the war then, and we still had a standing army of over three hundred thousand men. All veterans."

"I can see how that'd made 'em a little touchy. But I don't think that's all that's botherin' that Mountie. He acted like he had some personal hate going against me."

Onderdonk shrugged again. "Perhaps not against you personally. Just against what you stand for. Most of the violent crime in Canada has come from American hardcases drifting north of the border. Sergeant Stuart has a particular hatred for American whiskey runners. He knows what they've done to the Indians. He wants Canadian law for Canadians. He will brook nothing that smacks of Yankee interference."

"Then they oughta put some more lawmen in here. One man . . ."

"Yes, the Mounties are stretched thin. Normally there is a detachment of a dozen men in this province, under an inspector named Sam Steele. A good man, Steele, but he had to take his detachment up into Alberta, where there are a thousand railroad workers striking. It's a very violent strike. To maintain order, Steele needs every man he can get. I'm just grateful he left Stuart here."

Raider noticed that the usually unflappable Onderdonk shuddered a bit when he mentioned the thousand strikers farther up the line. They were, of course, another contractor's worry, but it wouldn't be impossible for the same thing to happen on Onderdonk's section of the line, and if it did, the delays and added expense would ruin him.

"Anyhow," Onderdonk said, "we're still having trouble with some of our Chinese workers. Have you gotten anywhere with that problem?"

Raider shook his head. "Haven't figured a way to get in with them yet. Real stand-offish bunch. Not that I can blame 'em. Not the way some of the men treat 'em."

"You'll have to try. The Chinese are my greatest worry right now. Without them, this line would not get built. I know the handicaps you're working under, Raider, but do your best."

"In spite of Sergeant Stuart?"

"Yes. In spite of Sergeant Stuart. I don't say that lightly, because, as chauvinistic a member of the British Empire as he may be, I respect him. The trouble is, he's only one man. He can't do it all, but he's too damned proud to ask for help. Particularly from Americans. Just do your best, Raider."

The interview was clearly over. Raider, annoyed, took his leave. He debated starting back up the trail toward the railroad. That was where the Chinese workers would be, not that it would help much. It seemed next to impossible for a Westerner to know what was going on in a Chinaman's mind. Real different people. At least they seemed different on the outside. Inside, maybe there'd be something in common to talk about. But how could he get inside, past all that understandable suspicion?

Raider decided the hell with it for now. It had been one hell of a long day, although not too unrewarding a one, despite tin-pot Sergeant Stuart. He knew for sure now that sabotage was actually going on. Not that he intended to kid himself that he'd completely ended it. He doubted those two yahoos he'd run off were anything other than hired hands. But at least now the saboteurs would know that their job was going to be a lot more dangerous than it had been before.

Raider headed for the nearest saloon. What he needed was a drink and a little relaxation. Maybe he'd even hole up in the hotel for the night and wait until tomorrow to do something about the Chinese.

The saloon consisted of a big bare room with sawdust on the floor, a plain plank bar, and a number of tables and chairs. As Raider bellied up to the bar, he was vaguely aware that a card game was under way at one of the rear tables. Blowing off steam playing poker might not be a bad idea. But first things first. He ordered a beer, drank it down in a few thirsty gulps, ordered a whiskey, drank that straight down, then proceeded to sip a second beer.

With the kinks now smoothed out, he glanced back to-

THE NORTHWEST RAILROAD WAR 59

ward the table with the card game and immediately became aware of a familiar voice calling out in glee. Goddamn, there he was, Happy Jack O'Reilly himself, leaning forward across the table, raking in a good-sized pot. Trust the little bastard to find out where they kept the money.

Raider wandered back toward the card game. Happy Jack flinched a little when he looked up and saw the big Pinkerton standing over him, but he quickly recovered. "Sit in with us," he said, waving toward an empty chair. "Your money'll do just as well as the next man's."

"The little bastard's luckier than any man's got a right to be," one of the other players snarled. Obviously a loser.

Raider took the empty chair, then placed a stack of money in front of him. It was Happy Jack's deal. He sailed the cards around the table expertly. The game was five-card draw. Raider was dealt two kings and some junk. He drew three cards. One of them was another king. He easily won the hand.

The deal moved around the table, past Raider, until it reached Happy Jack again. There were four other men playing besides Raider and Happy Jack. Since Raider had sat in on the game, there had been few winners except himself and Happy Jack. Once again, Raider tried to catch the little gambler cheating, but could not.

Happy Jack began his deal, the cards flicking smoothly out to each player. Once again Raider found himself with a damned good hand. Apparently it was not the only good hand, because betting was fierce. The man who had made the earlier crack about Happy Jack's luck was one of the fiercest bettors. Not that he had much choice. He was down toward the end of his stake, and would have to win this hand or fold. He was a huge man, running somewhat to fat, but the massive slope of his shoulders indicated there was a lot of muscle beneath the surface blubber. His name was McGee.

McGee took two cards. He didn't have much of a poker face; Raider saw McGee's eyes bulge when he looked at the cards he'd drawn. When the betting came around his way, McGee not only met the ten dollars bet, but raised the bet with his last twenty dollars.

Raider met the thirty dollars, and so did the men after him. Happy Jack looked worriedly at his hand, then even more worriedly in the direction of McGee's hand, then finally raised the pot another thirty dollars. Two men folded. Now it was up to McGee to see the bet or fold. The problem was, he had already bet all his money. Glowering at Happy Jack, McGee reached around behind him and jerked out a huge knife. Happy Jack's eyes widened when he saw the knife, and he started to back away from the table, but McGee only laughed, although it was a strained, ugly laugh. "No, I ain't gonna cut your guts out, bucko," he said. "Not yet, anyhow. I'm puttin' up my knife to cover the bet—and to raise it another fifty bucks."

It was indeed a handsome knife, with a long blade tapering to a needle point, the kind called an Arkansas toothpick. The grip was ivory, and the hilt seemed to be worked in gold. A handsome weapon, Raider decided. But the game was getting too rich for his blood; sure as hell too rich for his three eights. He folded. So did the two men after him. The game was now between Happy Jack and McGee. Happy Jack hesitated for a moment over accepting the betting value McGee had placed on his knife, but knew better than to push the argument too far. Not with a man like McGee.

Happy Jack put up his money and called. McGee, grinning triumphantly, threw down his hand. "Full house! Aces and queens!"

He was actually leaning forward to rake in the pot when Happy Jack held up his hand and shook his head. McGee sat back in his chair, an ugly scowl on his already ugly face. "Straight flush," Happy Jack said as he expertly fanned his cards out onto the tabletop.

A look of incredulous disbelief twisted McGee's features, followed a moment later by a look of pure hatred. "Why, you cheatin' little shit!" he bellowed. "Ain't no mealymouthed card-shark gonna make a fool outta me.

You want my knife? Well, slicker, you kin have it...right up your gizzard!"

Happy Jack let out a frightened squeak as McGee seized him by his silk foulard tie and dragged him halfway across the table. McGee's right hand scrabbled through the money and scooped up the Arkansas toothpick. He drew it back, obviously blind-mad enough to shove it right through Happy Jack's chubby little body.

Raider, who was sitting to McGee's left, drew his .44 in one smooth motion. Placing the muzzle about a foot from McGee's head, he thumbed back the hammer. Even in his rage McGee had no trouble recognizing the rather distinctive sound of a pistol being cocked. He froze. "Put the knife away," Raider said in a soft but hard voice. "I hate gettin' blood all over my cards."

McGee slowly turned his eyes toward Raider, then his whole bullet-shaped head swiveled on its thick neck. His little pig eyes glared crazily, but the big hole in the end of the Remington's muzzle was awfully convincing. The knife thudded down onto the tabletop, and McGee took several steps backwards, until he was next to the wall. Still seated, Raider slid the big pistol back into its holster.

McGee looked wildly back and forth from Raider to Happy Jack, who was now feverishly raking in his pot, including the knife. "I see it all now," McGee said in a hoarse, rasping voice. "You two work together. I heard the little weasel invite you into the game. You feed each other cards. Then when somebody catches on, out comes the hardware."

Raider was beginning to feel thoroughly annoyed. He didn't like being accused of cheating. Not only was it a personal insult, but having a reputation as a card cheat was not particularly healthy in a construction camp filled with hard men. If he did nothing about it...

"Seems to me you were the one who brought out the hardware first," he said, his voice level.

"Don't try gettin' out of it," McGee snarled. "You're a dirty son of a bitch of a lyin' cardsharp. If you was any kind of man at all, you'd get rid of that piece you're packin' and meet me bare-handed, man to man."

There was a murmur of approval from many of the men in the saloon. They had formed up into a half circle. Raider could see from their faces that they might already be wondering if there was some truth in what McGee was saying. That was bad. He'd gained some points earlier in the day by bringing in the wagon wreckers. The fickle winds of public opinion might be about to run him right out of the area. That would sure as hell make Sergeant Stuart happy.

Maybe it was the thought of Sergeant Stuart's contemptuous manner that did it, maybe it was mounting exasperation, or maybe it was simply the string of continuing insults McGee was pouring out. Raider abruptly stood up. For a moment his right hand hovered near the smooth walnut grips of his .44. McGee paled and fell silent. Then Raider began unbuckling his gunbelt. When it was off, and he was holding it in his hand, he looked up at McGee. "Tell you what, big-mouth. You an' me, we'll go outside and settle this man to man. The winner takes that last pot."

Happy Jack let out a bleat of financial agony. "Shut up, you little grifter," Raider snarled. "I just saved you from wearin' that toad-sticker in your wishbone, real permanent-like. One more sound outta you . . ."

Happy Jack obediently shut up. McGee, grinning, led the way toward the front door. There was a growing roar of approval from the other men. One drunk who had been draped limply over the bar looked up blearily and asked what was happening. Another man pointed to Raider. "This here stranger's gonna fight Big Bull McGee."

Raider groaned inwardly. He hated fighting men named Bull; it usually involved a whole hell of a lot of pain. Nevertheless, he was committed, so he followed McGee out the door—which almost ended the fight right there, because the moment McGee was out in the open, he spun around and charged back toward the doorway, hoping to trap Raider half inside and finish him off quickly.

Since this was not exactly Raider's first barroom brawl,

he awoke to the danger in time to roll quickly to his right, his shoulder hitting the dirt while McGee grabbed at empty air. Raider was on his feet before the other man could recove and move toward him.

They were now both out in the open, two big men, carefully circling, each looking for an opening. They were of about the same height, but McGee outweighted Raider by perhaps as much as fifty or sixty pounds. How much of it was fat was another question, but those extra pounds were going to be hard to move against.

A growing circle of men ringed the two combatants. Raider could hear bets being taken. One of the voices seemed to be Happy Jack's, and he was betting on McGee. Happy Jack was no sentimentalist.

McGee, tiring of the cautious circling, attacked first, throwing a wicked kick at Raider's shin. Raider sensed the kick coming and slid his leg out of the way, and then McGee was moving in fast over the kick, rushing forward with the intention of seizing Raider in a headlock, then battering his face with his free hand.

Raider shifted to the right and snapped a hard left into McGee's meaty face, followed by a walloping right to the other man's ribs. McGee chuffed heavily for a moment and clapped his hand to his ribs, which was when Raider should have rushed in to punish him more, but his boot heel caught on a rock and he had to windmill his arms to regain his balance.

McGee was on him like a maddened buffalo, running in fast, head down, his arms pistoning out and up with terrible force. Raider was able to catch most of the blows with his forearms, which hurt like hell, deadening his arms from fists to shoulders, but some of the blow got inside, two of them hitting him in the chest, knocking the wind out of him, while one hit high on his cheekbone, fortunately only a glancing blow, but it split the skin, and now Raider was bleeding.

The sight of Raider's blood seemed to madden McGee even further, and he kept pressing in, still pumping wildly with those huge arms. But with his head down he couldn't see where he was going, and Raider was able to raise a knee up into the other man's face. Raider heard McGee's nose break, and when he stepped back, there was blood on his jeans, McGee's blood. And now it was Raider's turn to go a little mad, but cool mad, and he began slamming blow after blow into McGee's face, quickly reducing it to a mass of raw hamburger.

With no apparent effect. As horrible as his face might look, McGee never faltered but kept charging in, and while his blows were wild, the ones that landed hurt. Raider knew that he could take only so many of those sledgehammer blows, while nothing at all seemed to faze McGee. He was probably the kind of man you could hit over the head with an ax and only dull the ax. A head like a cannonball.

Then Raider remembered the beginning of the fight, when he'd hooked one into McGee's ribs and McGee had faltered for a moment. Maybe that was the answer.

Raider began hammering McGee's ribs, a relentless series of blows, using, as much as possible, the points of his knuckles. It obviously hurt. McGee slowly began to curl up, and his breath was now wheezing noisily in and out of his nostrils. Down came the hands, to protect those tender ribs, and now McGee's face was completely without cover. So far Raider had only been able to hammer the man's forehead and nose and cheeks. Now the chin was totally exposed.

Raider noticed that McGee's teeth were tightly clenched as he fought the pain in his body. Raider punched hard, one hand after the other, punching *down,* straight against the point of McGee's unguarded chin. McGee's bullet head jerked sharply, the leverage of that heavy double blow to the chin rattling his brains.

Big Bull McGee's eyes rolled up in his head and he staggered wildly. One last choking gasp came from deep inside his chest, and then he suddenly collapsed like a felled tree. He hit the ground and didn't move again, just lay there, out like a light, his breath snoring noisily in and out of his half-open mouth.

Raider staggered away. Only now was he beginning to realize in how many places he hurt. Men crowded in close, laughing, slapping him on the back. He needed those slaps like he needed a bullet in the head. He pushed free of the throng, and then saw Happy Jack standing in front of him. For once there was a semi-serious look on the little man's face. "I'm in your debt," he said to Raider. Then he turned and vanished into the crowd.

Someone thrust a half-full bottle of whiskey into Raider's hand. He took a big drink. The whiskey stung cuts inside his mouth, his body ached, he wanted to rest. He started back toward the bar to reclaim his gunbelt, maybe to have a beer to soothe his parched throat.

As he stepped up onto the wooden porch, he caught sight of a glimpse of scarlet about fifty yards away. Looking up, he saw Sergeant Stuart, staring straight back at him. Even at this distance Raider couldn't mistake the look of undisguised contempt on the Mountie's humorless face. Angry, Raider turned away and pushed in through the saloon doors. God, he felt awful.

CHAPTER EIGHT

Raider spent the night in the hotel after all. And part of the next day. He woke up with a ferocious hangover; there had been a wild post-fight celebration in the saloon. Raider hadn't been able to buy himself a drink—men had shoved glass after glass into his hand. Raider shuddered as he remembered the huge amount of frontier rotgut he had imbibed.

He also ached from head to foot from his fight with Bull McGee. His arms and his rib cage were particularly bruised, covered with big yellow and black and blue welts from McGee's massive fists. It took until noon for the pain to smooth out a little.

Raider was a little annoyed with himself. My God! Getting in a fight over Happy Jack O'Reilly! But he couldn't have just stood by while Bull McGee knifed the little bastard.

Of course, he'd let McGee rile him, get under his skin. Admit it, he'd been ready to fight. Not McGee, but that sanctimonious Mountie, Stuart. How he'd have liked to plant a fist right in the middle of that grim, disapproving face—which, of course, he could not do, not as long as he wanted to remain in British Columbia.

Actually, the fight turned out to have done Raider some good. The next afternoon, when he finally exited the hotel, he found men everywhere who wanted to buy him a drink, or slap him on the back, or just stand and talk. He was a celebrity. Yesterday he'd not only brought in the two yahoos who had wrecked the freight wagons, but he had also beaten Big Bull McGee in a toe-to-toe fight. The men seemed more impressed with his victory over McGee than with his corralling of the saboteurs.

Everyone seemed to have forgotten about his face-off with Sergeant Stuart. Or maybe they were simply too polite to mention it. Well, time to get to work, time to deal with the problems Onderdonk was having with the Chinese workmen. Raider stopped by the railroad office to get more facts from Haney, then he loaded his trail gear on his horse and headed out of town.

He could have stayed in the hotel another night; after all, he wouldn't be able to reach the construction camps before dark anyhow. But he was tired of Fort Yale, tired of people. From the beginning he had been aware of the incredible beauty of this northern land, but up until now all his attention had been on the progress of the railroad, the hunt for saboteurs.

Raider headed up into the mountains, away from the railroad line. Almost immediately the silence of the wilderness closed around him. It was not a dead silence, but rather the absence of the noises of man. The wind soughed softly through the big spruce and pines trees. Squirrels chattered. Birds broke into song or argued with their neighbors. A small stream splashed noisily over waterworn rocks. In the clear, thin air, sounds carried for miles.

So did the eye. He rode down the slope of a mountain. There was a broad valley a few miles ahead, blue with distance, and beyond the valley, rising abruptly, a range of saw-toothed mountains, their highest peaks glinting with residual snow. Flowers brushed past his horse's hooves: paintbrush, aster, arnica, lupine, valerian. The sweet smell of crushed grass and petals rose up around horse and rider.

He rode down into the valley, past aspen trees, with their striated bark and quivering leaves. Tiger lilies thrust up heavy, yellow, nodding heads. On the side of the next mountian he encountered ponderosa pine. The ground beneath the pines was clean of everything but their own fallen needles. The trees' sap discouraged other life. Selfish bastards, Raider thought.

About an hour before dark he sighted a good place to spend the night, a low spot on the far side of a long meadow. The meadow was covered with sweet grass and fuzzy, white, ball-shaped flowers. Raider rode across the meadow toward a fast-flowing stream. He finally stopped in a small depression near the water, bordered by flowering arbutus and broom. There was an exceptionally beautiful view. Across the stream another broad meadow reached toward a line of low trees and, beyond the trees, gently rising hills.

Out of habit, Raider had chosen the site as much for security as for its beauty. There was an unclimbable cutbank at his back. In front, the stream was too deep and rapid to easily ford; it would be very difficult for anyone to move up on him unseen. Besides, the little depression in which he planned to camp would make him difficult to see.

Raider unsaddled his horse, replacing the bit and reins with a soft horsehair hackamore that would let the animal feed more easily. He attached a long rope to the hackamore and pegged the other end in a place where there was plenty of good grass.

Within another five minutes Raider had found sufficient firewood, and a short time later had a small fire going. On impulse, he took a line and hook out of his saddlebags. Digging down into the sod, he quickly captured some large red worms, which he used to bait the hook. Sitting on the soft grassy bank, he trolled the hook downstream. Within three minutes he had caught a good-sized trout. Another ten minutes brought him its twin, and half an hour later Raider was feasting on pan-fried trout and trapper's biscuits, which had been baked over the fire in the same pan in which he'd fried the trout. Cold clear stream water was his only drink.

Fed, but not overfull, Raider stretched out his bedroll and lay down, watching the last of the light go. The distant tree line went first, then the rising hills. Light lingered on the surface of the water for a little while longer, and longest of all, on the peaks of the faraway mountains.

Raider laid his Winchester next to his bedroll, the muzzle propped a few inches off the ground on some low twigs. His .44 went into the bedroll with him, close at hand. He'd made the bedroll himself, several years before, out of some old overcoats he'd bought for a dime. He'd covered the wool with waterproof oilskin, against rain. It made a snug, warm nest, with flaps to pull up around his face when the cold was at its bitterest. The bedroll, which the American cowboys called a soogan, had not been washed since it had been made. From time to time, when he felt he was no longer living alone in his soogan, Raider used the old Indian ant-blanket method of cleaning, pegging the bedroll down over an anthill for a couple of days, until the hungry ants had cleaned out any uninvited insect life.

A small blackened hole in the top of the bedroll was a testimonial to the good sense of remaining armed, even in bed. A couple of years ago a killer Raider had been tracking had tried to turn the tables, and had tracked Raider, crawling up on his camp while he slept. Raider shot the bandit through the bedroll just as he was bending over to cut Raider's throat.

Snug, secure, and fed, Raider lay awake awhile, watching the stars come out. Slowly, the last of the light faded, until it was completely dark. In the clear mountain air the stars spread across the sky in a great glittering bowl. The Milky Way cut a broad creamy path directly overhead.

There was so much starshine that it was possible to make out features of the surrounding terrain.

Something moved once, out on the meadow on the other side of the stream. Raider's hand drifted down toward the butt of his .44. Then he relaxed. It was only a buck deer. The buck snorted, perhaps picking up the man-scent, then raced away, bounding gracefully across the grassy meadow.

Raider finally let himself fall asleep. He slept as he always slept on the trail, restfully but lightly, his senses constantly alert for any sound that might warn him of danger. When he slept in a room, in a town, he snored horribly, much to the regret of anyone who might be sharing the room with him. On the trail, where silence might mean the difference between life and death, he did not snore at all. His breathing was quiet and even.

Raider woke at first light. He had brought along some eggs from town. Building another small smokeless fire, he quickly fried them. Normally he did not make coffee on the trail; the strong odor was too much of a giveaway, but this morning, doubting that anyone was after him—not yet, anyhow—he brewed up a small pot.

Not being in any hurry, he lollygagged around camp, killing time, washing in the stream. The icy water soothed the bruises he'd picked up in the fight with McGee. He didn't ride out until after ten o'clock, late for him when he was on the trail, but still earlier than he'd been accustomed to begin his day when he'd been living in Miss Livonia's establishment.

It was a long ride, and he took it slowly. He noticed that the mountains still abounded in wildlife. That would change, of course, when man the killer moved into the area in greater numbers. He saw lynx and bobcat, fox, marmot, and, amazingly, a few beaver working industriously in a pond, planning their winter. He caught a glimpse of a bighorn sheep standing sentinel on a distant crag. As soon as Raider's head topped the ridge line the animal abruptly disappeared.

When the sun had passed the middle of the sky, he came across a huge bull moose, tearing plants out of a large pond. The moose looked grumpily in Raider's direction, obviously annoyed. Raider nodded, spoke a low "Howdy," and continued on his way. Peace-loving men did not trifle with mooses. Or was it meese?

Raider reached the rail line with only a couple of hours of daylight left, but that was the way he wanted it. For the time being he preferred not to be too visible, but rather to be the one doing the watching.

It was not difficult to locate the part of the camp where the Chinese lived, an area of crude log huts cramped closely together. The Chinese workers were not exactly swamped with luxury. That was, of course, one of the factors that prompted contractors to hire them: the lack of frills. Haney had told Raider about the problems Onderdonk had had before finally deciding to import coolies. He'd always had a labor shortage; British Columbia, a sparsely populated land, was short of manpower. Bringing men in from eastern Canada was very difficult; they had to be brought in via the United States, a roundabout and costly process, which was the main reason the railroad was being built: to connect the eastern and western parts of the country.

At first, large numbers of men had been brought up from San Francisco. The results had not been good. Most of the men who came north had nothing much going for them in the States—roughnecks, gamblers, thugs, men on the run. For the most part, they had been more trouble than they were worth.

Running out of money, and desperate, Onderdonk remembered how well coolie labor had worked out during the building of the Central Pacific across the United States. So, over the outraged cries of the local whites, he had sent for the coolies, ship after ship full of them, thousands of men, mostly from Kwang Tung province in the south of China.

Onderdonk had been delighted with his Chinese navvies. The very first batch had been ordered to proceed about thirty miles up into the mountains, where they would work. To Onderdonk's amazement the coolies simply picked up their packs, started walking, and by that night had not only arrived at the work site but had already set up a neat camp. The next morning they got up early, ate a quick meal, and were ready to work. To move a camp of protesting, drunken, irritable white men the same distance would have taken a week.

Which of course was one of the reasons the whites hated the Chinese so much. They did a prodigious amount of work, and they did it honestly and with little trouble. They didn't get drunk, or at least not often. In comparison, the white workers were a quarrelsome, drunken, lazy lot. Worst of all, from the white point of view, the Chinese were willing to work for less money, which caused the white men to fear for their own wages. Attacks on Chinese by whites were very common.

Keeping out of sight, Raider rode into a small wood that gave him a good view of the Chinese camp. There was not much activity around the Chinese huts, except for two cooks, already beginning to prepare the evening meal. Raider knew that a camp of white workers lay just over the hill, but he had so far seen no other white men in the area besides himself.

He remained in the woods for another two hours, chewing some jerky, watching. Finally, as the shadows grew long, a large gang of coolies came into sight, shovels and picks over their shoulders, marching back to their camp. One of them walked a few paces ahead, and since he didn't carry any tools, and wore clean clothing, Raider figured he must be the gang's "book man," their connection to the Five Companies, the Chinese contractors who had arranged their passage to North America. Raider studied the book man, the way he walked, what he could see of his face. The book man might be his only passport into the world of the coolie, the only one who spoke English or had any idea of what the Occidental world was about.

THE NORTHWEST RAILROAD WAR 73

Just before dark Raider was surprised to see two white men slip into the Chinese camp. "Slip" was the right word: they seemed to be moving furtively. Pulling out his binoculars, Raider studied their faces. He didn't remember having seen them before. They disappeared into one of the huts. About an hour later they left the camp, still moving furtively.

Raider decided to follow. Staying a couple of hundred yards behind, he had no trouble avoiding detection; the way the two moved through the woods suggested to Raider that they were city men rather than men used to the wilderness.

They led him straight to the camp where the white workers were quartered. Watching through his binoculars from about a hundred yards away, Raider saw the two men approach several workmen seated outside a large tent. At first it appeared that the newcomers were not particularly welcome—until they produced a couple of bottles of what appeared to be whiskey. The men around the tent began to drink, and soon the scene was boisterous. Raider watched as one of the men who'd come from the Chinese camp said something to the others. At first they seemed to disbelieve him, voices were raised in protest, but the man continued to talk insistently.

Raider changed his position, moving closer, until he was able to hear. "I tell ya, I seen it with my own eyes," the man was saying loudly. "Them slant-eyed bastards got 'em two white women over there. An' from what I seen, them two ladies ain't at all happy about bein' there. My guess is that they were snatched somewheres, and forced to go along with them Chinks."

The men's earlier disbelief was slowly being replaced by anger. "Kidnapped, you say?" a workman shouted.

One of the men who'd brought the whiskey nodded vigorously. "An' if I don't miss my guess, that's the last the world's gonna see of them two young ladies... once the Chinks get through with 'em. You know how a Chinaman can make a body disappear."

He didn't elaborate, but apparently the members of his audience were creating vivid enough images in their own minds. "We gotta get them girls outta there!" a man shouted. He was answered by a chorus of yells, and a moment later the white camp was in motion, men picking up pick handles, axes, anything that came to hand. A few had pistols.

Raider immediately went back to his horse, swung up into the saddle, then headed straight for the Chinese camp. Being mounted, he arrived well before the white workers. The sound of his horse brought most of the Chinese out of their huts. Raider looked around for the book man, slid down from his horse, and walked up to him. "You got trouble comin'," he said. "A big mob of white men, headin' this way."

Raider was totally unable to read the expression on the man's face. He was wondering if the book man understood English after all when he finally asked, "Why?"

"They think you've kidnapped some white women and are holding them against their will."

"Why do they think that?"

"The two white men who left this camp about an hour ago just told them so."

"But . . . it isn't true! There are no women here!"

"You know that, and I'm pretty sure I know that, but there's one hell of a lot of other hombres who sure as shootin' don't, an' in about five minutes more they're gonna be here, ready to kill."

The Chinese was silent for a few seconds. His eyes, inscrutable to Raider, carefully appraised the big Pinkerton. "And you are here to help us?"

"Yep."

"How? What can we do?"

"Get the men out into the open. All of 'em. Get 'em around the fire."

The book man spent perhaps another five seconds appraising Raider, then turned quickly and began issuing quick, decisive-sounding orders in Chinese. Within another twenty seconds, coolies were pouring out of their huts.

Meanwhile, Raider had led his horse into some trees, out of sight. He then came over and sat down at the fire next to the coolies, directly across from the book man.

"My name is Lee Fat," the book man said.

"Raider."

"Just Raider? I thought all Westerners had at least two names."

"Just Raider."

There was a moment's pause. "Why do you help us?"

"So there won't be trouble. I work for Onderdonk. He wants this railroad built. He figures someone is tryin' to stop it."

Lee Fat said nothing. A moment later they could all hear the shouts of the white mob as it approached. Some of the coolies, looking alarmed, started to get up. "Tell them to stay put," Raider said to Lee.

Lee spoke sharply. The men subsided, but Raider could see that many had brought their tools with them, pick handles and axes, like the men in the white mob. He saw no evidence of firearms.

A moment later the mob erupted into the firelight. "Let's get the bastards!" someone shouted, and the mob surged forward—until the ones in front noticed Raider, a white man, seated peacefully in the midst of the Chinese.

The forward movement stopped. It was the incongruity of Raider's presence, more than anything else, that caused the men to falter. They were prepared to see screaming, mutilated, violated white women, half-remembered images of their own sisters and sweethearts, at the mercy of the heathen Chinese. But here was a man more or less like them, sitting quietly, sipping a cup of tea.

Raider looked up. "Hello, gents. What brings you over this way?"

"Hey," someone called out. "He's the guy who beat Big Bull McGee."

"An' brought in those wagon wreckers," another added.

One man stepped forward. Raider recognized him immediately, it not by face, then by type. The mob leader type.

"What the hell are you doin' here, mister?"

Raider held up his tin cup. "Havin' a cup of tea."

"I mean . . . with these here Chinamen?"

Raider held up his cup again. "The Chinese make damn good tea." Actually, he detested tea.

The mob leader looked uneasy, but with all those men behind him, he had to ask. "Where's the women?"

"What women?" Raider replied, obviously puzzled.

"The white women these heathen bastards kidnapped!"

"Yeah," another man shouted. "The one's they're rapin'!"

Raider looked all around him. "Well, if you ask me," he finally said, "it's one hell of a dull rape."

"You mean there ain't no white women here?" the mob leader demanded.

"Nope. Been here an hour or so. An' if there was any women—white, yellow, red, or black—I'd have noticed. Been out here in these woods long enough to kinda . . . well, to kinda think a lot about women."

Some of the men laughed. The mob leader, sensing that he was going to be cheated out of a night's fun, grew angry. "Maybe there's women here, and they're bein' hid," he said truculently. "Maybe you're—"

Raider stood up abruptly, in one smooth powerful motion, and a second later his face was only a few inches from the face of the man who'd challenged him. "You callin' me a liar?" he asked, his voice dangerously low. "You tryin' to say that I'd be pimpin' for these men? Or for anybody at all?"

Looking into Raider's eyes, the cold blackness of them, the man's courage abruptly took off on a long trip. "Well, I . . ."

"If you've been told there was women here, white women, then why the hell don't you ask the men who told you? Have 'em show you where they are—or where they were—instead of runnin' around in the night, spoilin' a man's cup o' tea?"

There was a mutter of approval from the mob, then a moment later a man called out. "They ain't with us no more. They musta skedaddled."

"Hell, I ain't seen 'em since we left our camp," another said.

Raider continued looking straight into the eyes of the mob's leader—former leader now, because there really wasn't a mob any longer, only a number of confused men, who wondered why they'd left their tents. They began to drift away. Raider turned and sat down again, across from Lee Fat, sipping tea from his cup until the last of the white men had disappeared from sight. Then he threw the rest of the tea into the fire. "You got any coffee?" he asked.

For the first time, Lee smiled. He said something to one of the cooks, who went off to make some coffee. Lee Fat continued to watch Raider until his coffee was brought to him, then Lee asked, "These men—the ones you said told the others we were harming white women—you are sure they were the ones who left this camp?"

"Positive."

Lee shook his head. "We were certain they were our friends. They..."

"They what?"

"Told us things. About how we were being cheated. How we were given the most dangerous jobs, and that was why so many of our people were being killed and injured."

"So they were stirrin' you up."

Lee slowly shook his head. "We thought they were right. We have been losing men. There have been accidents, bad food..."

"I think I know the kind of accidents. Powder charges goin' off at the wrong time, banks cavin' in, rotten food. It's been happenin' for a while, and not just to you Chinese."

"It has been done on purpose?"

"I wouldn't be surprised if most of your trouble was 'arranged' by those two hombres that tried to sick those navvies onto you. We've already caught some others."

Lee was silent for a while. Finally he spoke. "I am ashamed. I, who am supposed to be here to protect the men, have been made to look like a fool."

"Don't blame yourself. There's been a lot of this going on."

Lee looked into the fire. "You have to understand... how difficult all this is for my people. They are all poor people from South China, from Kwang Tung. Poor farmers, who would have had no chance of ever changing their life if they had remained in China. They come here with one hope: to save the incredible fortune of three hundred American dollars, so that they can return home rich men. But so few do. By the time they arrive here, they already owe the Five Companies forty dollars for their passage. Then they must buy their food at the construction company's store... for very high prices. They must also buy their own tools, and clothing, and medicine, if they are sick, although most simply die when they become sick. All of this comes out of a wage of one dollar a day. And there is no work in the wintertime, so our people are lucky to save forty dollars a *year*. This work will not last long enough for most of our people to save even what they need to return to China, as poor men. Poorer than when they left."

"Well, yeah," Raider said uncomfortably.

Now Lee Fat showed his first real emotion. "Ah! I make myself sick!" he said disgustedly. "I am crying like a baby."

He looked up at Raider, his eyes hard. "We are proud men. We do our work and we do it well. We do not lie, we do not cheat, we do not steal. We obey both our white foremen and the men from the Five Companies. But if anyone cheats us, if they play with out lives... then we make certain that they pay for it."

Raider nodded. He knew that Lee Fat was right. On occasion some of the more stupid foremen had tried to cheat the coolies out of a portion of their wages, or to force them to work under unusually dangerous conditions. The results had been instant riots, with some badly battered foremen.

Lee Fat stood up. "We thank you," he said abruptly. "We are in your debt. But for now we would like you to leave."

"Well, I . . ."

Raider noticed that about half the men were missing. "Where . . . ?" he started to ask, then he heard some shouting from off in the darkness. A moment later several coolies entered the firelight, leading one of the men who had tried to sic the mob onto them. Lee Fat had a quick conference with his men, then turned to Raider. "I sent them out a while ago. Earlier in the day one of our men saw where this one and his companion were camping. Unfortunately, the other one got away. But we have this one."

"Then let me take him with me," Raider said. "I've got a lot of questions that need answering."

Lee Fat shook his head. "No. He is ours."

"I need him. I need to hear what he has to say," Raider said stubbornly.

Lee Fat shook his head again. "We owe you our thanks. But if you insist on this, our gratitude will no longer exist. Go. Go now, before you see things that you should not see."

Recognizing the implacable will in those narrowed Oriental eyes, Raider could only nod. One of the men had brought him his horse. He mounted and started to ride away.

The man being held by the Chinese tried to break free, to follow him. "You gonna leave me here with these heathen animals?" he cried out frantically.

Raider turned back toward him. "You made your bed. Now sleep in it."

And as Raider rode off into the darkness, and heard the first awful scream, he had no doubt it would be a very long sleep.

CHAPTER NINE

As far as Raider was able to detect, there were no visible repercussions over the revenge the Chinese had wreaked on the man who had betrayed them. Lee Fat would have made certain of that. No doubt there was now a body buried under several tons of railroad right-of-way dirt fill.

Raider continued to ride a circuit of the construction zone, a large area, almost a hundred miles long, up the valley of the Fraser River. He was an increasingly visible presence. While he had not told anyone but Lee Fat that he was working for Onderdonk, the general understanding among the workmen was that he was. And that any move against the railroad would most likely meet with a lot of grief as long as Raider was around.

For more than a week after the incident with the Chinese, there were no further acts of sabotage against the railroad. Haney was delighted, quite noisily so. Onderdonk was delighted too, but in his usual quiet, restrained way.

Then early one evening, when Raider was relaxing in

Fort Yale after a meeting with Haney and Onderdonk, the lull in the action came to a halt.

It began with a familiar face. Raider didn't pay much attention to the man at first. He seemed to be just another navvie, dressed pretty much the same as the other workmen, wearing battered low-heeled boots, a flannel shirt, and loose trousers held up by heavy suspenders. What was wrong about the man's appearance was that his clothing, while far from the latest in fashion, was neither ragged nor particularly sweat-stained. This was not a man who earned his bread by heavy labor. Yet he was not dressed as a gambler or businessman either. Raider's attention had been drawn to the man simply because he didn't fit into any of the local categories.

And then Raider recognized him. It was the survivor, the other man who had tried to sic the white miners onto the Chinese, the one who had gotten away.

Raider had been sitting well back in the shade, on the veranda of a saloon. He was fairly sure that the man had not seen him, so when the man disappeared around a corner, Raider quickly got up and followed him.

Following someone, and not having them know they were being followed, was not an easy trick in Fort Yale— it was simply too small a place. It was a particularly difficult operation for a man who stood out against his background as sharply as Raider.

He let the man build up a big lead, while he kept back in the shadows as much as possible. Finally he saw the man go into a rooming house. There was no question of following him inside; he'd be spotted immediately. Keeping other buildings between himself and the rooming house, Raider finally found a location off to one side where he could keep an eye on the rear as well as the front entrance of the building.

His forethought was rewarded about ten minutes later when the man he was following came out of the rooming house's rear door, accompanied by another man. It was beginning to grow dark, dark enough so that Raider could barely make out the faces of the two men, but as far as he could tell, he had never seen the second man before.

The two men proceeded toward the edge of town. For a moment Raider thought they might be leaving the area, but he quickly realized that was unlikely, since both men were on foot, and neither looked like men who would walk when they could ride.

It was now fairly dark. Raider found himself following the men almost as much by ear as by sight. He had to get closer. Fortunately, there were a great many stumps and low bushes in this area, so he was able to close the distance to about fifty yards, moving carefully from cover to cover.

The men were traveling in a loose half circle, and the circle seemed to be taking them toward Michael Haney's nitroglycerin plant. Haney had pointed the plant out to Raider with great pride. With all the tunnels to be built, and all the roadway to be blasted out, Onderdonk's project naturally ate up a great deal of explosives. With freight charges so high, and communication with the outside world so poor, securing a supply of a volatile explosive like nitroglycerin was not easy. Haney, once he had been called onto the job, solved the problem by simply building a nitro factory. So far it had produced several tons of the touchy and powerful explosive.

For one tense moment, Raider suspected that the two men were about to blow up the nitro factory. No, that didn't make sense, they were too damned close. If all that nitro went up, they'd go up with it.

The factory was dark, its workers gone for the night. Raider watched the two men slip inside. Raider hesitated, not at all anxious to rush in after them. If they got nervous, if he startled them, there might be shooting, and with all that nitro in there . . .

Five minutes later the men reappeared, carrying a box. Nitro, it had to be full of nitro.

Raider followed the two men back to the rooming house. A couple of minutes later a light appeared in a second-floor window. Raider continued his vigil. About an hour later the light went out. When the men failed to reappear, Raider concluded that they must be sleeping.

Raider headed for the livery stable, where he saddled his horse and loaded the animal with his trail gear. Taking his horse with him, he then chose a position on a small hill at the edge of town, about two hundred yards from the rooming house, where he could keep the building under observation through his binoculars.

Raider continued watching the rooming house all night. At dawn, the two men once again left by the back door, one of them carrying the box they'd removed from the explosives factory.

Now it was their turn to visit the livery stable. Twenty minutes later, mounted, they rode out of town. One of the men held the box balanced on the cantle of his saddle, and from the care he took to shield the box from accidental jolts, Raider now had no doubt at all that it contained nitro.

The big question was, What were they going to do with that much nitro? Whatever, Raider doubted they were out for a day of innocent fun.

And what was Raider going to do? The night before he'd mulled over the idea of playing it straight, of going to Sergeant Stuart and telling him about the stolen nitro. There were two things wrong with that idea. The first was that he wasn't sure that Sergeant Stuart would cooperate with him. The second was that, as far as Raider knew, Sergeant Stuart was not even in the area. There'd been talk that the Mountie'd been called away up into the interior over some trouble between the local Indians and some farmers whom the Indians had accused of encroaching on Indians lands. Once again, there was no local law available.

Raider continued to follow the two men. It was fully light now, so he had to stay well back. At this point his options were unclear. He doubted the wisdom of riding up to the men and simply accusing them of theft. With so much nitro being produced daily, how could the box they were carrying be adequately identified? It would be his word against theirs. Besides, he wanted to find a way to nail them both for something more serious than theft.

Nothing to do but follow. It was ten in the morning before the two men rode their horses up onto a small hill and stopped. The hill looked down onto the rail line, and since it was lightly wooded on its forward side, the two riders could see downward without being easily seen from below.

There was a great deal of activity down by the line. Men were grading roadbed, others were laying down ties and ballast, while still others were bringing up wagonloads of steel rails.

At this point, as at so many other points along Onderdonk's stretch of track, the rails ran very close to the side of a mountain. A sheer slope rose up several hundred feet above the roadbed. The slope didn't look very stable; slides would be a common occurrence in an area such as this. Accordingly, a large party of men were hard at work on an avalanche shed, a long structure with a sloping roof, built out from the mountainside over the track, the whole thing constructed of heavy logs that would, hopefully, protect the track from falling rocks and debris.

Raider swung his binoculars back onto the two men sitting their horses on the little hilltop. One of them pointed down to the construction site, then up to the sheer mountain slope above it. His arm went higher, pointing to an outcrop about five hundred feet up. Raider saw the other man laugh, then pat the box of nitro in front of him. There was little doubt in Raider's mind what they meant to do. Blow that overhang down onto the track—and onto the men working below.

The men left the hilltop, heading toward the mountain. Raider could see that there was no easy way up there, not to the overhang that seemed to interest them so much. They'd have to take a circuitous route, ride the long way around. Fortunately, Raider was actually closer to the mountain than they were. Gambling that the overhang was in fact their destination, Raider immediately kicked up his horse and headed toward the mountain.

It was a close race, with Raider having to work hard, both to make good time and to make certain that the men didn't see him. He was helped by the fact that he wasn't headed for the overhang itself, but for a small flat spot that lay a couple of hundred yards above the only trail that would take the men to where they wanted to go.

Raider was riding a very heavily lathered mount by the time he made it to the little meadow he'd seen from below. Tying the horse well back out of sight, he took his rifle from its scabbard, then carefully crawled forward to the edge of a little flat spot.

About five minutes later the two men came into view, below Raider, toiling up the trail, their horses as lathered as his own. "Goddamn it, Jake!" one complained to the other. "How we gonna get back down once we touch off the nitro?"

Jake pointed ahead along the trail. "Goes down the other side. We just keep on ridin'."

They pulled their horses to a stop and dismounted. The only way they could get close to the overhang, close enough to plant a charge that would bring it down onto the men working below, was up a narrow trail. Too narrow and too steep for horses.

The as yet unnamed man got down stiffly, grousing to Jake about his saddle sores.

"Just shut up an' think of all the goddamned money we're gonna make off this one," Jake replied irritably.

"If we get to spend it. Charlie didn't get to spend a penny o' his money after those Chinks caught him."

Jake shuddered, so strongly that Raider was able to see it from where he was watching. "Jesus! I wonder what they did to him. Never did find no body. Joe was so pissed off when he heard about it... wanted to go after the dude he thinks tipped off the Chinks."

"That big guy?"

"Yeah. The one who pounded the shit outta Bull

McGee, an' ran Pete and Little Willy outta town, after that wagon thing."

The other man shook his head. "I can't figure out why Joe just don't go after him, wipe him out once an' for all."

Jake snorted. "Well shit, use your brains. If we did it real open like that, then that dumb Mountie'd know for sure there was somethin' goin' on, an' then they might bring a whole lotta other law in here. Uh-uh. Joe wants to take care of that Raider hombre the quiet way ... unless he keeps causin' trouble."

The two men were toiling up the trail, which was rather steep. The man carrying the nitro called a halt, then put down the box, wiping his brow. "Stuff's heavy. Well, the box is, anyhow. Besides, maybe we better fix the fuse down here where it's fairly flat. Once we get up on that overhang..."

"Yeah. We'll be hangin' by our fingernails. There must be easier ways of makin' a livin'."

"Not likely," the other man said, laughing.

The two men were almost directly below Raider now, maybe a hundred yards away. He watched the one who'd been carrying the box squat next to it, then pry off the lid. Sticking one hand gingerly inside, he pulled out some blasting caps, complete with fuse. The man sat back on his heels, pulled out a big clasp knife, and carefully trimmed a length of fuse. Next, he began attaching the fuse to the blasting caps.

While the man was at work on his fuses, Raider slowly crawled closer, until he was only about eighty yards away, at the very edge of a ledge, a little higher than the two men. As quietly as possible, he slid his rifle forward. He normally kept the rifle sighted in at about a hundred yards, so he knew he wouldn't have to adjust the range. Nor was there much wind, so he wouldn't have to allow for windage, especially with the heavy bullets his Centennial threw.

Below him, the last fuse had been connected, and the man doing the work carefully placed the fuses back in the box with the nitro, then stood up, dusting off his hands. "Well, that does it. Now," he said, jerking his thumb in the direction of the rough trail they would have to climb, "as long as we don't drop the fuckin' stuff."

Jake laughed, a rather tense laugh, then all laughter ceased as Raider jacked a round into the chamber of his Winchester. Under the circumstances, it was a horribly loud sound, a deadly ca-*chunk,* ca-*chunk,* which instantly brought both men to their feet. Raider had an impression of shocked faces staring up at him but paid them little attention because he was not aiming at either of the men. He was aiming at the box full of nitroglycerin.

Jake and his companion were horribly aware of Raider's target. That long barrel was lined up straight at the deadly box at their feet. They'd have been less terror-stricken if Raider had been aiming at them.

"Noooooo!" Jake screamed, turning to run. The other man tried to run too, but they were both too late. The big rifle fired, slamming the butt back against Raider's shoulder, jarring his body. An instant later the massive bullet slammed into the box, splintered its wooden sides, then ploughed through its contents—the fuses, the sensitive blasting caps, the even more sensitive nitro.

The trail erupted into a pillar of flame, dust, and smoke. Raider rolled back over his ridge just in time, hugging the dirt while stones and clods of earth whizzed through the air above him. When he finally looked up, he saw that there was now a shallow pit in the middle of the trail. The brush for dozens of yards around was shredded. Of Jake or his companion there was at first no sign. Finally, Raider thought he saw a charred bundle of rags lying about forty yards away. Or maybe it was only part of a charred bundle, because there was something else burnt and messy-looking lying off another twenty yards, too small to be a whole man. Having a somewhat touchy stomach, Raider did not stay to investigate. No one out in the open, as Jake and his buddy had been, could have survived such an explosion.

Raider's horse had been spooked by the blast. He had to

gentle the animal before he was able to mount. Once in the saddle, he headed down toward the trail, intending to head out the way Jake had suggested.

After he reached the trail, he saw another bundle of rags off in the opposite direction from the first two. No telling whether it was Jake or the other man.

Well, as they'd been saying about Charlie, neither one of them was going to be able to enjoy spending any of that easy money.

CHAPTER TEN

Once again, relative peace returned to the rail line. Raider figured that maybe whoever was masterminding the sabotage was running low on men. So far he'd taken out five.

Raider was back in Fort Yale a few days later, lounging on the front veranda of a saloon, nursing a drink, when he caught sight of Sergeant Stuart marching down the street. Raider had little doubt the Mountie was looking for him; Stuart walked straight up onto the veranda and sat down a couple of feet away. Amazing. Raider had never expected to see Sergeant Stuart do anything as human as sitting down.

"I see that you're still here," Sergeant Stuart said coolly.

"You got good eyes."

A whole minute of silence followed. Sergeant Stuart finally spoke. "There are some interesting rumors coming out of the Chinese work camps."

"I wouldn't know. I don't speak Chinese."

"And two men were killed in an explosion the other day."

"That ain't unusual around here."

"This wasn't a construction accident. It looks like the two men were planning... well, I'm not sure what they were planning."

"Who were they?"

"We can't tell. There wasn't enough of them left to identify. It occurred to me that you might have some information as to their identity."

For just a moment Raider was tempted to tell what he knew. He was accustomed to working *with* the law rather than in spite of it. It would be a damned big help to have the Mountie on his side. He was within an inch of confiding in Sergeant Stuart... until he turned and looked into the Mountie's eyes. Those icy gray eyes. And Raider realized that Sergeant Stuart was perhaps more interested in nailing Raider than in getting at the truth. "Nope. Don't know a thing," Raider said flatly.

If possible, Sergeant Stuart's eyes grew even colder. "You're walking on thin ice, mister. I won't have—*we* won't have—men like you breaking the peace here in Canada. You Americans..."

Raider and the Mountie were staring one another straight in the eye. Neither would look away. Finally, a noise in the street gave them both the chance, and they looked away at exactly the same moment. No face lost.

Sergeant Stuart abruptly stood up. "Remember what I said. Watch your behavior," were his parting words, and he stalked off, back ramrod stiff, uniform immaculate, boots highly polished, white cork sun helmet tipped slightly over his eyes, its brass chin strap perfectly positioned. Her Imperial Majesty Queen Victoria's loyal soldier-man to the core.

Raider stared after the Mountie. All this interview had done was reconfirm that so far he'd been playing it the right way. He'd have to continue to work quietly. It was clear that something more than a love of the law was eating Sergeant Stuart; Raider couldn't get over the feeling that Stuart was holding something personal against him, some kind of grudge. Or maybe he just plain hated anybody from south of the border.

"Walks like he's got a poker up his ass, don't he?" a voice said from a few feet away. Raider turned his head. A man was standing near the doorway into the saloon. Raider recognized him as one of the regulars, a steady drinker.

"He used to be an officer in the fuckin' British army," the man continued."That's where he gets all that spit and polish stuff. Always was a rigid bastard."

"You sound like you know him."

The man nodded. "I ought to. Served with him for three years."

Raider took a closer look at the man. He was a seedy-looking specimen, half drunk as usual, but, on closer inspection, there was a residual toughness under the present ruin. "You were in the Mounties?" he asked.

The man nodded solemnly. "Yep. Don't look like it now, do I? But I was in the outfit right from the start. Joined up with the first of 'em, back in '73."

Suspecting he'd run across a likely vein of information, Raider shoved out a chair with his foot. "Take a load off your feet and set a spell. I'd like to hear about the Mounties."

As the man sat down, his eyes drifted toward the half-full bottle of whiskey on Raider's table. Raider obligingly filled his glass. The man drank half the glass down in one long thirsty gulp, as if afraid that someone might take the whiskey away from him. Raider lazily waved toward the bottle, and the man filled his glass to the top again.

He introduced himself as Pat. "I was outta work back in '73, when they decided to form the Mounties. The country was only a couple of years old then, an' the politicians, bein' politicians, started worryin'. All of a sudden they were runnin' one of the biggest countries in the world, land-wise, and most of that land, the part out west, was practically empty, nothin' there except Indians, and a few trappers and traders workin' for the Hudson's Bay Company. And there was all those Yankees down south, lookin' for new lands to fill up. That's when the politicians got the idea of settin' up the Northwest Mounted Police. Some men to ride herd on all that empty ground, 'fore somebody else took it away from Canada."

"Sounds like a big job. And the Mounties don't seem too big on manpower," Raider cut in.

"Nope. Never were. Started out with only three hundred men—to bring law and order to an area bigger than Western Europe. And by God, we did it, too!"

Pat launched into a series of anecdotes, some personal, each pretty much the same: small parties of Mounties, often less than half a dozen, facing down bandits, rumrunners, and angry Indians, usually successfully, usually without firing a shot. "There was a sayin', then, that the Mounties didn't scare worth a cent. Still true."

"I take it you aren't a Mountie anymore."

Pat nodded with a sharp jerk of his chin. "Nope. Quit 'bout eight or nine years back."

"How come? Sounds like you kinda liked it."

Pat pursed his lips thoughtfully. "Liked it? Well, I don't know if I'd exactly put it that way. I suppose what it boils down to is that I like the idea of havin' *been* a Mountie. Gives me some good stories to tell. Gets me one hell of a lot of free drinks."

He raised his glass, which was nearly empty again. Raider nodded for him to refill it. "You see," Pat said. "For most of us rank-and-file Mounties, it was a real dull life. We lived way out in the middle o' nowheres, usually in barracks, with a buncha other Mounties, no women, usually freezing our asses off in the winter an' fightin' bugs in the summer. An' then there was all that discipline, all that military-type stuff. Men like Douglas Stuart, well, they eat up that kinda thing. I don't know why he left the British army, but he tried to bring all that crap here to Canada with him. That man made my life a livin' hell. The time I got drunk an' run off for a week with that chief's daughter..."

A distant smile stole over Pat's face as he relived an old

memory. "The march," he suddenly said. "That first march, when all three hundred of us took off for the Northwest Territories, marchin' across those plains and into the mountains. Took us months to get where we were goin'. The horses died like flies, and we thought we were goin' to starve to death. Most of us had never been out there before, and we couldn't understand how it could be so big. It wasn't long before most of us looked like somethin' the cat dragged in—boots worn out, holes in our uniforms, shaggy as mountain men. But not Douglas Stuart. He was only a corporal then, but you coulda mistook him for a fuckin' general, he was so damned shiny and perfect. Yep. That man's got a poker up his ass, all right."

"He don't seem to like Americans much."

"Nope. He sure as hell don't."

"Why?"

Pat, who was quite drunk by now, stared off into the distance, his eyes not quite focusing. "He's seen some pretty bad things," he muttered. "We all seen some things you Americans did. The whiskey runners..."

Pat's head slumped down onto the tabletop, and in a few seconds he was snoring. Raider sipped a little more of his whiskey, then he got up, ready to go back to his hotel. So, he hadn't been wrong about Stuart. The man had a hard-on against Americans. Raider had made the right move in not trying to reason with him. Where there was that much anger, there was no reasoning. He'd have to keep going it alone.

A few days later, when Raider was resting his horse alongside the railroad right-of-way, he received his first tip-off. One of the coolies passed close by and, without turning his head, hissed, "Lee Fat. Want see you."

"Where?" Raider replied softly, also without turning his head.

"Forrow me."

Raider mounted and trailed after the man, keeping far

enough back so that he did not seem to be following. A couple of hundred yards later he found Lee Fat standing in a little hollow out of sight of the rest of the camp. Raider swung down from his mount. "How's it going, Lee Fat?"

Lee Fat looked thoughtfully at Raider's extended hand, then finally shook it, at the same time giving a small but graceful bow. "I have information," he said.

"What kind?"

"The kind that might help the railroad. Maybe about trouble coming."

"How'd you come across this information?"

Lee Fat shrugged. "You know that there are very many Chinese people here. But the white barbar... white men ... often do not even notice us, do not think we have ears or eyes or the normal feelings a man has. So they talk in front of us as if we were not there. Some of them were talking yesterday, where one of my people, who speaks a little English, heard things. Things about causing more trouble."

"What kind of trouble?"

Lee Fat shook his head. "I do not really know. The Chinese man, he does not have very much English. But he knew enough to know that they were planning violence. And he knew enough to know that they were talking about the *Skuzzy*."

"Skuzzy?"

"The boat. The one that Mr. Onderdonk uses on the upper part of the river, to bring supplies to the railhead. I think they are going to wreck the *Skuzzy*."

"When? How?"

"Don't know how, but maybe when. My man thinks they were talking about today."

"Damn! Where the hell is the boat now?"

"Only five miles downriver, taking on a load of logs. If you hurry..."

"Thanks, Lee Fat. I'm on my way."

Raider swung into the saddle, but Lee Fat stepped in front of his horse. "Raider, you must understand. The

Skuzzy means a lot to the Chinese people who work here. When Mr. Onderdonk bought the boat, everyone said he would not be able to get it up the river. Water too rough. More than one time he tried to run it past the rapids at Hell's Gate, but each time the boat was pushed back by the water. Finally, it was the Chinese who did it—and an American pilot. One hundred fifty coolies walked along the cliffs above Hell's Gate, pulling ropes attached to the *Skuzzy*. It was very hard work, very dangerous, we could have fallen off those cliffs, but we did it, we pulled the boat past the rapids. Now the boat does good work, and we are proud of it; it is partly our boat now. We do not want to see it wrecked. You stop those men, huh, Raider?"

Raider nodded and galloped away. It was a short run to where the boat was moored. He made it in good time, the *Skuzzy* had not yet cast off. It was not a very large boat, less than a hundred and thirty feet long. The rigorous run up and down the upper Fraser, with its rocks and rapids and narrow channels, had beat the hell out of the little steamer. A lot of paint was missing, and the planking on its sides was scarred and split by minor collisions. But the *Skuzzy* still floated.

Raider left his horse back in the trees, then did his best to approach the boat without making a big show of it. The *Skuzzy* was just casting off. He jumped aboard seconds before the gangway was pulled in.

"Just made it, buddy," a crewman said.

"Where's the captain?" Raider demanded. "I have to see him."

"Why, he's up in the wheelhouse, an' he's real busy right now, mister. This ain't no easy river to navigate."

Indeed, the *Skuzzy* was already under way, the big stern wheel churning, driving the boat out into the narrow channel. Raider could feel the powerful current pulling at the hull. Nevertheless, he insisted that the crewman take him to the captain.

The captain was not happy to have the privacy of his wheelhouse invaded. "What the hell are you doing in here?" he snarled, his big hands firm on the wheel, never taking his eyes off the channel ahead.

"I've heard a rumor that someone wants to wreck your boat."

The captain's eyes narrowed, and for a moment he glanced at Raider. "Where'd you hear that?"

"From a good source. Now, tell me, are there any passengers aboard?"

"Why, yes. Three men came on board about ten minutes ago."

"Workmen?"

"Well, now that you mention it, no. Hard-lookin' men. I was of a mind not to let them board, but we had the space."

"Where are they now? I didn't see anyone on deck."

"Well, that's where they're supposed to be. I'll tell you what. You go down with Dick, here, an' he'll show you around. There's no way I can leave the wheelhouse right now."

Raider nodded, and a moment later he and Dick were leaving. "Ain't never an easy minute," the captain groused after them. "It ain't enough that the river's always tryin' to wreck this old girl, now some yahoos have to try it too."

Dick took Raider on a quick tour of the boat. There was no sign of the three men in any of the public areas. "Where else could they be?" Raider asked.

"Well, in with the cargo, but you can see that all of it's right out here on deck, in the open. Nowhere to hide. The only other place is—"

"—the engine room!" both Raider and Dick said together.

Raider moved quickly toward the gangway that led into the engine room. Dick lagged behind a moment to pick up a marlinespike, a piece of metal about eighteen inches long, used for splicing cable. His lagging behind probably saved them both. Just as Raider stepped into the passageway, a man moved out of the darkness behind him and covered him with a pistol. "Hold it right there, pilgrim," the man snarled.

Raider was considering whether or not to chance turning around and going for the man when he heard a loud yelp of pain behind him, followed by the thud of a falling body. Turning, Raider saw Dick standing a few feet away, holding the marlinespike, which he'd just used on the man's skull.

The man's pistol had fallen to the deck. Raider picked it up and tossed it to Dick. "Cover him," he snapped, then he pulled out his own pistol and raced down the passageway toward the engine-room door.

When he poked his head around the doorway he saw the grease-stained body of the engineer lying prone upon the deck. The engineer's head was bloody. Another man was doing something to the engine, while another covered the doorway with a pistol. The moment the man with the pistol caught sight of Raider, he fired. Raider ducked back barely in time. The bullet gouged splinters out of the door frame, some of them stinging Raider's face.

Flattening himself against the wall, Raider pondered his options. There was little point in trying to get into the engine room through that doorway. With a man inside covering the entrance it would be suicide.

He raced back to where he'd left Dick and the man Dick had hit. The man was sitting up now, groaning and holding his head. Dick was standing nearby, pointing the man's pistol at him. "On your feet," Raider snarled, jerking the man up from the deck, which brought another groan. For a moment the man's eyes refused to focus, then they finally looked onto Raider. "You!" he said, "If we'd known you'd be here . . ."

"What the hell's going on in the engine room?" Raider snarled. "What are those men doing in there?"

The man started to smile, then the smile quickly faded. "Hey, we gotta get off this boat!"

"Why? What's happening?"

"They're stoking up the boiler and tying down the safety valve. When the pressure builds up enough, this old tub's gonna blow itself right out of the water."

Raider had seen boilers blow on riverboats before. The results were usually disastrous, sometimes totally destroying the entire boat.

"How were you going to get off the boat before it blew?" Raider demanded.

The man pointed toward a lifeboat a few yards away. "We were goin' in that."

The lifeboat lay out in the open on the deck. Now that they had been discovered, there was no easy way for the men below to reach it. The man Raider and Dick had captured realized this. "Hey! I mean it. We gotta get outta here 'fore this old tub blows!"

"Uh-uh. We're stayin' aboard."

"But—"

"Shut up. Now get movin'. You walk ahead."

Raider pushed the man ahead of him down the passageway. Dick followed about two yards behind. When they reached the doorway into the engine room, Raider shouted, "You in there. We know what you're planning. Open up the steam valves and bleed off that extra pressure, then come on out with your hands up."

"Fuck you, mister!" someone shouted from inside the engine room. A moment later there was a shot, and a bullet gouged a hole in the passageway wall, not far from where Raider was standing.

Dick had crowded closer. "Jesus! I can hear the steam valves hissin'. They're loadin' up fast."

"Yeah. Well, we're goin' on in."

"You can't. They'll shoot the first man through that door."

"Maybe. But I ain't gonna be first."

Raider's statement alarmed Dick—until he saw that Raider was pushing their captive toward the doorway. "No! Wait a minute!" the man shouted, struggling wildly, but

Raider clouted him lightly on the back of the head with his gun barrel, then pushed him through the doorway ahead of himself. Almost instantly a gun roared, and Raider heard the bullet smack into the man's body. He'd figured whoever was in there wouldn't open up on one of their own, but it looked like he'd been wrong.

As the man toppled into the engine room, clutching his chest, Raider ran in through the doorway, immediately moving to one side, barely in time, as a bullet flew by his head, missing him by less than an inch. He caught a glimpse of the man who'd fired, crouched several yards away, half hidden behind some machinery. Raider snapped a shot in that direction. His bullet ricocheted wildly off the machinery. The man yelped and ducked away, out of sight.

"What's happening in there?" Dick called out from the doorway.

"It's clear for the moment. Come on through."

Dick ran in through the doorway, quickly hunting cover. He looked down at the man who'd been hit. He was no longer moving, and Raider suspected that he was dead. "The safety valve," Dick said nervously, staring toward the big steam engine.

"Try and get to it. I'll cover you."

Dick nodded, swallowed nervously, then made a run for the valve. Raider fired three fast shots with his .44, the bullets ricocheting off metal engine parts. The angry buzz of the bullets did their job, keeping down the heads of the men hiding farther back in the engine room. Dick reached the valve and slammed it open. Almost immediately the valve began venting steam, noisily, jets of white vapor screaming up the stack toward the open air.

Raider thought he heard a sound from the rear of the engine room, a sound like a heavy door or hatch slamming, but it was difficult to be sure over the noise of the steam. "Is there another way out of here?" he shouted to Dick.

"Yep. Small hatch that leads up on deck."

"Okay. You keep watch here. I'm going outside."

Raider ran back down the passageway, out onto the open deck. A quick glance showed him an armed man climbing a ladder toward the pilothouse. Real hardworking sons of bitches, Raider thought. If they can't wreck the *Skuzzy* one way, they'll do it another.

Raider shot the man off the ladder, but even as the man was falling, a second man fired from well back on the deck, narrowly missing Raider. Raider rolled behind a lifeboat, then rolled out the other side into the open, snapping off a shot at a shadowy figure. The man ducked back out of sight.

For the next five minutes it was cat and mouse, with Raider playing the part of the cat. He moved steadily forward, dodging from cover to cover, firing, reloading, firing, reloading, driving the man further back toward the stern of the boat.

Finally, amidst the clutter of the heavily loaded deck, Raider lost sight of his quarry. Hugging the deck, he was just starting around a stack of lumber when he heard the sound of a pistol being cocked somewhere above him. Rolling over onto his back, Raider now saw where the gunman had gone—he was up on the superstructure, right above Raider, hanging on to the smokestack with one hand, aiming his pistol at Raider with the other.

Raider desperately tried to bring his pistol around to bear, but he knew he was going to be too late. Then suddenly two pistols roared almost together, the gunman's a split second after the other. The gunman's body jerked under the impact of a bullet, and his own shot went wild, gouging splinters out of the deck only inches from Raider's head. The gunman tried to hang on to the smokestack, but slowly his hold loosened. The pistol went first, falling from weakening fingers, then a moment later the man fell, his body smashing into a pile of machinery.

Rolling to his feet, Raider saw Dick standing farther back along the deck, a smoking pistol in his hand. "I decided to come up on deck," Dick said apologetically.

Raider looked over at the dead gunman, then at the place where the gunman's bullet had hit. He remembered waiting for that bullet to plow into his body. He turned toward Dick and shrugged. "Hell, I ain't complainin'."

CHAPTER ELEVEN

When the *Skuzzy* put in at its next stop, the bodies of the saboteurs were taken ashore. Naturally, a crowd formed, and in an amazingly short time various accounts of what had happened aboard the little steamer were spreading throughout the work camps, accounts which were for the most part even more colorful than the actual events.

Before the boat docked, Raider had already gone through the pockets of the three dead men. He found nothing that would give him any clues as to who had employed them, no pattern that would lead him to the ringleaders. Once again there had been no survivors to question.

Naturally, the news reached Sergeant Stuart, too. Late that afternoon the Mountie strode into the mess hall where Raider was eating a late lunch. There was quite a crowd of admiring workers around Raider; he was finding it difficult to eat his meal in peace. Some of the men were questioning him on the details of the gunfight aboard the *Skuzzy*, others, the hangers-on, were working away at back-slapping, while still others were looking somewhat askance at

Raider. In the eyes of this latter group, a rather different image of the big stranger was emerging—not so much an image of Raider as a guardian of the law, but rather as a lethal weapon, a frightening engine of destruction.

Sergeant Stuart pushed his way through the crowd. "Oh shit," Raider muttered into his plate.

Shouldering the last man aside, Sergeant Stuart stood over Raider. "You're under arrest," the Mountie said, tight-lipped.

"I'm . . . what?"

"If you'd like it put more formally, you're to be held for an inquest and investigation into the shootings aboard the *Skuzzy*."

"Arrested? Hell, what's got into you, Stuart? It was a clear case of self-defense. I was defending both me and the boat."

There were shouts of approval from several of the men. Sergeant Stuart seemed unmoved. "If it was self-defense, the inquest will bring that out, which is what an inquest is for. Now, if you'll kindly stand up and hand over your weapon."

There were growls of disapproval from the spectators. Raider continued to sit for another few seconds, looking up from under his eyebrows at the Mountie. Priggish son of a bitch, he thought. For a moment he was tempted to tell Sergeant Stuart that if he wanted his weapons, he was welcome to try and take them. But this was Canada, he was a foreigner, and Sergeant Stuart was the law.

Standing up slowly, Raider reached a hand down toward the butt of his .44. Sergeant Stuart did not move at all, simply remained standing, obviously waiting for Raider to hand him his pistol. Arrogant bastard, Raider reflected. Used to obedience from a well-trained population. I wonder how long he'd last in Texas, or Montana?

Nevertheless, Raider simply handed the Mountie his pistol. That seemed to satisfy Sergeant Stuart; he did not ask Raider to hand over his bowie. The pistol was symbol enough of his domination over the other man.

104 J. D. HARDIN

Sergeant Stuart took Raider to Fort Yale, the two men riding together side by side over the Cariboo Wagon Road, neither saying a word. They camped out for one night, conversing only when absolutely necessary. When they reached Fort Yale, Sergeant Stuart discovered that the area's head jurist, Mathew Begbie, Chief Justice of British Columbia, was in town, holding court. "This will save us riding all the way down to New Westminster," Sergeant Stuart said, obviously pleased. "We'll go before Judge Begbie immediately. He probably will be able to conduct the inquest without any delay."

"I hope he's better company than you are," Raider grumbled.

The Provincial Chief Justice was certainly *impressive* company. Judge Mathew Begbie was a very big man, pushing six and a half feet tall, heavily built, handsome, bearded, and well-dressed. He exuded an aura of strength, intelligence, and determination. When he looked up at Raider, Raider at first thought the man's eyes had a somewhat sleepy look. Then he noticed that the apparent sleepiness appeared to be made up of a combination of good humor and intensity of purpose. Not a man you'd try to hand a phony story.

When Raider and Sergeant Stuart entered the courtroom, Begbie had been about to leave; the day's hearings were already over. But, seeing Stuart with Raider, Begbie sat down again behind his desk. "What have you brought me this time, Sergeant?" he asked Stuart.

"Three men were killed aboard the *Skuzzy*. This man shot them."

"I shot two of them. One of the *Skuzzy*'s crewmen shot the third man," Raider corrected.

Sergeant Stuart looked slightly unsettled. "Why didn't you tell me that earlier?" he demanded.

"You never asked me. You were too goddamned eager to arrest me."

"Hold on . . . hold on," the judge said, with a slight edge

to his voice. "I want to know everything that happened. In detail."

Raider studied Begbie for a moment. Finally he decided that the judge might be a man with whom one could reason, a refreshing change after having repeatedly locked horns with Sergeant Stuart. So Raider told him most of the story, told him, at least, about Onderdonk's earlier suspicions about sabotage, and how he, Raider, had been doing his best to stop it. He told him about catching the wagon wreckers, and the details of the fight aboard the *Skuzzy*. When he had finished, Sergeant Stuart added his suspicions about the man who had disappeared among the Chinese, and the strange explosion in the mountains that had killed two other men.

When both had finished, Begbie steepled his fingers together. "It sounds as though you've been a busy man, Raider. Let me ask you just one thing. When you ran across these... saboteurs, and saw them engaged in their nefarious work, did it ever occur to you to take these matters to the local law?"

"Couldn't find the local law," Raider replied, noticing Sergeant Stuart's face go red. "Every time, things were just... happening. It's a big lonely place out there. I had to make a decision either to act on the spot or forget about it."

"Mmmm... I see." Begbie looked down at his steepled fingers, then looked up suddenly, his eyes pinning Raider. Nope, not a man to give a line of crap to. "So... you say you're working for Mr. Onderdonk."

"Well, not exactly."

"Then who do you work for?"

"The Pinkerton National Detective Agency."

"Damn!" Sergeant Stuart burst out, using the first profanity Raider had ever heard pass the impeccable Mountie's lips. "A Pinkerton!"

Begbie looked at Sergeant Stuart quizzically, as if rather startled to hear so much vehemence coming from a man usually so controlled.

Then Begbie turned back to Raider. "I don't know yet

just how I feel about a member of your agency operating here in British Columbia. I'll have to think about that for a little while. But I do know one thing."

The judge tapped his fingertips against his desk top. "As far as the matter of the killings aboard the *Skuzzy*, well, if what you both tell me is true, then there was nothing else you could have done. Any less, and the *Skuzzy* would have been lost, along with the men aboard her. I can only commend you on a job well done, Raider."

"Thanks, Judge."

Begbie's eyebrows raised. "By the way, how did you come to suspect—"

"I was tipped off."

"May I ask who tipped you off?"

Raider shook his head. "Nope. If I told you or anybody else, there could be trouble for the man who warned me, and if that got around, well, that'd be the end of tip-offs. Let's just say that the man who told me had the best interests of the railroad at heart."

Sergeant Stuart made an exasperated sound. Judge Begbie looked at him coldly. Sergeant Stuart subsided. "Case dismissed," Begbie said curtly. Sergeant Stuart, red in the face, looked like he wanted to say something, but Begbie forestalled him. "Sergeant Stuart," he said reprovingly. "We all appreciate the job you do here in British Columbia, particularly since, for the past few weeks, you have had virtually no one to help you. But perhaps in the future you might try a little harder to fight against letting your personal prejudices overcome your good judgment."

Sergeant Stuart's facial color faded from red to white. Not the white of fear, but the white of a combination of anger and shock almost too great to bear. He managed to utter some sort of strangled assent, then spun on his heel and marched from the room. Raider was about to follow him out, but Judge Begbie asked him to remain. "In other times, more normal times, when the imposition of law and order has a greater number of willing and well-trained hands to help it along, I might have asked you to leave the territory, simply in the interests of maintaining good order. But there does seem to be a problem here after all. I had heard earlier of Mr. Onderdonk's suspicions about possible sabotage. I asked Sergeant Stuart to investigate. He assured me that there was no basis to the allegations. Now, I wonder if perhaps Sergeant Stuart's, um, antipathy towards Americans might not have colored his judgment. He definitely does not like Americans, as you may have noticed."

"Yeah. I figured that out a while ago."

"His feelings are not unique. Many here in British Columbia feel that the province is being taken over by Americans and Chinese. Not a very enlightened viewpoint, I'm afraid, but there it is."

"Yep. Sometimes railroads cost a lot more than just money."

The judge nodded. "An interesting insight."

He stood up, quite a towering column of manhood. "Well, on your way then. I think you can consider the matter of the shootings on the *Skuzzy* safely behind you now."

"Thanks, Judge."

But as Raider turned to go, Judge Begbie called out after him. "Raider, maybe the next time you run across some of the same kind of trouble ... maybe you might try to find a way of letting the local authorities know first, before you manufacture any more dead bodies."

CHAPTER TWELVE

Deciding that it might be a good idea to lie low for a few days, Raider rode to a small town situated in a narrow valley about two hours' ride from the railway. The sale of alcohol was not permitted within twenty miles of the construction area, which, Raider considered, was not too bad an idea. Construction men tended to get violent when they drank, and violent, drunken men didn't get much railroad building done.

This particular town lay just outside the dry zone, so it was an attractive destination for men with some time off, which at this point included Raider. After his confrontation with Sergeant Stuart and Judge Begbie, Raider was in the mood for a drink, and in this little town he found a large and prospering saloon, which suited him just fine. The saloon also had a couple of reasonably attractive barmaids. Raider, lounging at the bar while he slowly worked his way through a bottle of surprisingly good whiskey, was wondering if the girls might dabble in other lines of work, perhaps professional endeavors involving more than the simple serving of drinks, something that might be more in line with the way he'd been living at Madame Livonia's.

Within an hour he'd begun to think that perhaps he'd run across some enthusiastic amateurs. From the warm smiles he was getting from one of the barmaids, a buxom brunette with huge, rather uptilted brown eyes and a high, fascinating bosom, there was a better than even chance that the exchange of money might not be necessary.

Unfortunately, Happy Jack O'Reilly was also in the bar, playing cards at a table toward the rear of the room. The little bastard seemed to show up just about everywhere. All Raider needed to wreck his day was to be saddled with another Happy Jack problem. Sometimes O'Reilly was more trouble than a roomful of confused badgers.

Happy Jack, however, after a brief nod in Raider's direction, seemed content to leave the big Pinkerton alone. At first Raider paid little attention to the little gambler, but within half an hour he began to get the definite impression that perhaps there was a little more to Happy Jack's behavior than simple politeness. Happy Jack seemed to be going out of his way to avoid looking in Raider's direction. Now why would he be doing that? Raider wondered.

Not that he intended to let that particular question dominate his thoughts. The brown-eyed barmaid, whose name was Cynthia, was responding nicely to his overtures, flashing him increasingly intimate smiles each time she passed by with another trayful of drinks. Yep. Tonight had all the earmarks of turning out to be one real fine night.

Until Happy Jack got up from his table and headed in Raider's direction. He did not walk straight up to him, but instead moved to a position at the bar about three feet away. Happy Jack rapped on the scarred bar top to get the bartender's attention, not—at least not openly—paying any attention at all to Raider. But Raider noticed that Happy Jack's eyes, which he could see clearly in the big mirror that lined the wall behind the bar, kept flicking sideways glances in his direction.

The bartender, a rather slovenly man, finally deigned to

notice Happy Jack. His sour look seeming to ask why Happy Jack didn't order his booze through the medium of one of the barmaids, he ambled over. Happy Jack ordered a whiskey, and the moment the bartender had walked away out of earshot, Happy Jack, talking out of the corner of his mouth, whispered to Raider, "I think there's some boys in here tonight gunning for you."

Raider continued looking straight into the mirror. For a moment he wondered if this were not one of Happy Jack's typical scams, but the worried look in the little man's eyes suggested differently. "Who? Where?" Raider murmured.

"A couple of mean-looking hombres sitting at a table near the side wall. There's one out in front, on the boardwalk, and maybe another one outside the back door, but I ain't sure about him."

"What makes you think they're after me?"

"I heard 'em talking earlier in the day. That's how I know there's four of 'em. They were all together, and now there's only the two sitting at that table. I heard one of 'em tell the other three that they knew you were headed this way, but that you weren't going to leave here alive. Something about having their orders."

Raider, lifting his eyes, and still looking into the mirror, studied the room. He saw two men sitting at a table in the area Happy Jack had indicated. They sure as hell did look like genuine hardcases. And both of them seemed to be staring at his back. "Thanks, Jack," he murmured to the little gambler.

"If there's anything I can do to help..."

"Just go on back and sit down. Hit the floor if any shootin' starts. And thanks for warning me."

"Nothing else I could do after the way you saved my bacon down in Fort Yale."

Well, so the little grifter had a conscience after all. Raider watched him covertly in the mirror as he picked up his drink and walked back to his table. Then Raider's eyes went back to the two men seated by the far wall. Not too bad a plan. They'd probably do something to goad him into

THE NORTHWEST RAILROAD WAR 111

a fight, then when the fight started, the two others would come into the bar from both the front and the rear and have him in a cross fire. He wouldn't stand much of a chance.

Except now he'd been warned, which changed the situation. Of course, the odds were still heavily against him, but if he made the right moves, he might be able to survive.

Still watching in the mirror, Raider saw one of the two men seated at the table nod to the other. Then they both began to rise to their feet.

Raider turned, and while his right side was hidden from the two men, he slipped the leather thong from the hammer of his Remington. Both men were on their feet now, one slightly in front of the other, both a little surprised to see that Raider was now facing in their direction, was, in fact, looking straight at them. They also noticed that his right hand was resting lightly against the butt of his .44.

They were even more surprised when Raider began to walk toward them. "Okay, boys," Raider said softly. "Better make your moves now, or get the hell out of here while you're still breathin'."

Raider had been moving to the side as he approached, so that the man in front almost hid the man behind. The man in front cursed, and both went for their guns.

They were both fast, but Raider was faster. His pistol was up, cocked, and leveled in one smooth motion, and he fired a split second before the man in front, his bullet taking the man in the chest. The man's shot went wild, shattering the mirror behind the bar. He grunted from the impact of the heavy slug, and was knocked backwards, toward the second man, ruining his chance for a clear shot.

The first man was a long time going down, taking a table with him as he fell, and as the other man struggled to move around the obstruction his companion's body made, Raider fired again, but his second shot was a little too rushed, and he only succeeded in creasing the man's neck. The wound sprayed blood, and the man flinched back, so that his shot went wild, missing Raider by more than a foot. Raider's next shot took him directly in the middle of the chest, and he too flew backwards, crashing through several chairs, hitting the floor only a second or two after his companion.

No matter how hot the action, Raider was in the habit of counting his shots. Like most men with single-action pistols, he always left the chamber under the hammer empty, to avoid accidental discharges. Which meant that he now had only two shots left.

And maybe two more live enemies. The man outside the front door had already shown in the doorway. Raider snapped a shot in his direction, gouging splinters from the door frame. The man yelped and ducked back outside, out of sight.

Raider spun to his left. The doorknob on the back door was turning. He fired through the door, high, in case he was mistaken as to who was there. He heard a yell from outside the door.

And then he shoved his .44 back into its holster and took a running dive forward, toward the fallen bodies of the two men he'd shot. He hit the floor, rolling, scooping up their pistols, one in each hand, continuing his roll until he had regained his feet.

He was barely in time. A man came rushing in through the front door, gun in hand, at almost the same moment that another man crashed in through the back.

Flattening himself against the wall, Raider opened fire with both pistols, hammering shots simultaneously to his left and his right. The newcomers were firing too, their bullets tearing holes in the wall behind him, but they were flustered, and shooting wildly. They had expected that, since they were coming at Raider from separate directions, he would only be able to face one of them at a time and the other would be able to shoot him in the back, but Raider continued to fire both of his captured pistols, one in each hand, careless of how much ammunition he wasted, firing rapidly, slamming shot after shot into the bodies of both men, the impact of the lead driving them back and doubling them up, until both were on the floor, bleeding, clearly no longer able to continue the fight.

Raider immediately dropped the two pistols he'd been using, then drew his own and quickly reloaded. Only then did the saloon's patrons begin poking their heads out from under the tables beneath which they'd dived the moment the first shot crashed out.

"God! Did you see that?" one man said in an awed voice. "Both hands. Firin' like two men rolled into one!"

His reloaded .44 in his right hand, Raider made a quick tour of the men he'd shot. They were all dead except for the one who'd come in through the front door. Hit three times, he didn't look like he'd be doing much more breathing.

The wounded man seemed to realize this himself. "Son of a bitch," he murmured as Raider knelt over him. "I shoulda know'd better. If Joe was so hot on this one, he shoulda done it hisself."

"Is Joe the man who sent you?"

"Yeah. I wish I had me one last shot at that slippery bastard."

"This Joe. What's his whole name?"

The man looked up at Raider. A moment's indecision showed in his eyes, then he apparently made up his mind. "I don't owe that bastard nothin'. Nothin' at all. His monicker's Devlin. Whiskey Joe Devlin. He's one real stinker."

"Where can I find him?"

But the man had begun to cough. Thick gouts of blood poured out of his mouth, choking him. His chest heaved several times then stopped moving, and Raider figured he'd cashed in his chips, but a moment later the man's eyes opened wide and he looked up at Raider. "You're good. Real good," he half whispered. Then a massive convulsion shook his body, and a moment later he'd stopped breathing permanently. His sightless eyes stared glassily up at the ceiling.

"Whiskey Joe Devlin," Raider murmured, standing up. "Don't mean a thing to me."

By now, everyone in the room was on his or her feet, including Cynthia, who was leaning against the bar, her face white, her right hand pressed tightly against her ample breasts.

Raider quickly holstered his .44, then headed toward the door. He had to pass Cynthia on the way. He looked into her frightened eyes and nodded regretfully. "Well, maybe some other time."

CHAPTER THIRTEEN

Raider had survived a gunfight, but he was not so sure about the aftermath. Judge Begbie was not going to be too happy about the latest tally of dead bodies. Neither was Sergeant Stuart. At the very least, he'd probably be asked, rather forcefully, to get the hell out of British Columbia.

He had a name to work with now, though—Whiskey Joe Devlin. He needed time to connect a man to that name. If he wanted to do that, he was going to have to be able to move around freely, which meant that he'd better not spend too much time in any one place. Particularly not here, near the scene of the gunfight.

Raider rode for the Fraser River, angling southwest. He reached the river just before nightfall, about ten miles below Fort Yale. He was lucky. A steamboat was about to weigh anchor and head downriver. He had no trouble boarding.

It was a moonlit night, and the steamer had no trouble navigating the river. It reached the mouth of the Fraser, and New Westminster, not long after dawn. No one paid much attention to Raider when he went ashore. He was not as well known in this area as he was farther upriver, in the construction zone.

Once ashore, he headed straight for the telegraph office. The main reason he'd come downriver was to use the telegraph before news of the shootings spread all over the territory. And so far the telegraph lines linking British Columbia to the United States went no further than New Westminster.

Raider sent a long telegram to the Chicago head office of the Pinkerton National Detective Agency, requesting information on one Whiskey Joe Devlin. The agency had the largest rogues gallery in the country. It contained the names and criminal histories of thousands of people, sometimes with accompanying photographs. Each name was carefully cross-indexed with information on the activities of anyone who had ever been unlucky enough to fall afoul of the law within hearing distance of the agency.

While waiting for the reply, Raider put his horse in a livery stable, then checked into a local hotel, washed, and caught up on his sleep. He checked back at the telegraph office late that afternoon, but there was as yet nothing waiting for him.

He spent a restless night. He'd finally gotten a lead on the man behind the sabotage, but he hardly felt he could go to the local law with the information. Not after the gunfight in the saloon. Saloon gunfights were a chancy business. It wasn't always that easy to assign blame or prove self-defense. There were already probably as many versions of the fight circulating throughout British Columbia as there had been patrons in the bar. The one thing Raider had going for him was the current lack of law in this part of the province. With luck, Sergeant Stuart would be off on one of his trips into the remote interior.

The next morning, Raider was at the telegraph office as soon as it opened. This time there was a long telegram waiting for him. "I'd hate to have to pay for this one," the clerk said, impressed.

THE NORTHWEST RAILROAD WAR 117

There were a couple of chairs along one wall. Raider sat in one and studied his telegram. Obviously the head office did have a file on Whiskey Joe Devlin. His history was not an exemplary one: he'd been in trouble with the law since he'd been a boy. He'd killed his first man at the age of seventeen. At least, that was his first reported killing. A year after that he'd served time for robbing a saloon. Later he'd gotten involved in the illegal whiskey trade in Canada, smuggling whiskey to the Canadian Indian tribes, hence his name, Whiskey Joe. The Canadians seemed to want him very badly. Perhaps that would give Raider an edge with Sergeant Stuart, when that hard-nosed Mountie finally showed up.

However, Raider would prefer to find his man himself. There would be a certain amount of satisfaction in turning the leader of the saboteurs, the saboteurs who were not supposed to exist, over to Judge Begbie and Sergeant Stuart. Let that priggish bastard Stuart put that in his pipe and smoke it.

Raider was perusing the telegram for a second time, seeing if he'd missed any information that might help him find Whiskey Joe, when the telegraph key started clattering again. Raider had got to his feet and was about to leave the office when the clerk called out, "Hey, mister. It's another one for you."

Raider went over to the counter. The clerk handed him the message. "Short one this time."

It was indeed short, another message from the head office, ordering him to immediatly cease all activities in British Columbia and return directly to Chicago. There were no explanations given, simply that curt order.

Never the most disciplined of operatives, Raider was damned if he'd let himself be pulled off the case just like that, especially when he'd finally begun to get somewhere. Angered, he sent back an equally simple reply, writing out on the message pad, "Go to hell." Then he paid, and left the telegraph office.

Back in his room he carefully studied the telegram containing Whiskey Joe's dossier, looking for information that might lead him to the man himself. Whiskey Joe's physical description was given in great detail. He was a little over medium height, with a powerful build, black hair, a ragged mustache, and dark eyes. There were distinguishing marks: Whiskey Joe was missing the third finger of his left hand, and his face was marked by a long curving scar on the right cheek, running from his ear down to the corner of his mouth, a memento from an outraged woman whom he'd let get too close to a razor.

Women. The report was full of references to Whiskey Joe and women. He constantly sought their company, but his brutal treatment of the opposite sex helped maintain a high turnover. The more Raider read, the more he became convinced that if Whiskey Joe was indeed in the area, the way to find him was through women.

From what was contained in the dossier, Whiskey Joe seemed most comfortable with dance-hall women, barmaids, and prostitutes, not that there were that many other types easily available in this lightly populated land.

Accordingly, Raider began his search in the local saloons, and hit pay dirt his very first night. "A man with a big scar on the right side of his face and a missing finger?" one dance-hall girl replied to Raider's question. "Yeah. I know him. Used to, anyhow, but I sure as hell hope I don't never see that son of a bitch again. Except maybe looking at him down the barrel of a shotgun."

Obviously her encounter with Whiskey Joe had not been a pleasant one, and her bitterness ran too deep for Raider to get much more out of her, but, encouraged, he kept on looking, widening his search area, and finally, about noon of the second day, he heard that Whiskey Joe might have been seen visiting a young woman in a nearby town called Granville.

New Westminster lay on a small peninsula that jutted out into the Strait of Georgia, with the Fraser River estuary at its southern border and a wide inlet of the sea to the north. New Westminster was located on the southern edge of the peninsula. Granville was about ten miles to the north, on the south shore of the ocean inlet, an easy ride. Raider set out immediately, reaching Granville in the early afternoon. He was lucky. The girl he'd been told about, a bar girl in a small saloon, was already at work. And when he asked her about a man with a scar, he got a definite reaction: the girl's face paled and she quickly turned away.

"I can see you know him," Raider said. "I'd like to know where to find him."

She remained facing three-quarters away from him, her shoulders hunched high, her hands working nervously. "I don't want to talk about him."

"I'll pay you for the information."

The girl shot him a quick look. "He's not the kind of man I'd like to cross," she said hesitantly.

"Twenty dollars. Just to tell me where I can find him."

She still hesitated. "Fifty," Raider said. That was one hell of a lot of money to pay out to a bar girl, but he knew that if he wanted to find Whiskey Joe, he'd have to do it soon.

The girl wrung her hands. "I . . . I'll have to think about it," she said nervously. "Come back tonight. Maybe about midnight."

That was the most Raider could get out of her. Figuring he was going to be here awhile, he stabled his horse and took a room. After that he spent some time looking around the area. Granville was a smallish town, just a couple of thousand people. It's main industry seemed to be saloons. There were sawmills across the inlet, but the area in which they were located was part of a dry zone, no liquor permitted, part of the Canadians' obsession with alcohol. But, loggers and mill workers being what they are, the men working across the inlet were going to have their liquor no matter what. An enterprising man named Gassy Jack had opened a saloon on empty land on the south shore of the inlet, and within a short time another enterprising man had started a ferry service, bringing hordes of thirsty workmen to Gassy Jack's liquor emporium. Within a short time a town had sprung up. One might say that Granville had been founded on a saloon.

But the local residents had higher hopes for their little burg. The city fathers were fighting to have Granville declared the western terminus of the new transcontinental railroad. Up until now the plan had been to locate the terminus way up at the head of the inlet, at Port Moody, a rather dismal little place with a mediocre harbor.

Granville's hopes were not unfounded. A couple of years before, the driving force behind the building of the railroad, a man named Van Horne, had gotten a good look at the magnificent harbor that opened out in front of little Granville. Van Horne had immediately declared that the town would make a wonderful railroad terminus and seaport. He even had a new name planned for his rail terminus—Vancouver.

Raider had to admit that it was a fine setting. Across the inlet, mountains rose sharply from a narrow coastal plain. Thick forests of huge red cedar trees covered most of the peninsula. A smaller peninsula that curved out into the inlet formed a natural harbor. A damned pretty place. Maybe someday Granville—or Vancouver—might amount to something.

Raider arrived at the saloon a little before midnight. If anything, the girl, whose name was Marie, seemed even more frightened. He tried to talk to her, but she refused to be drawn into conversation. "Not out here in front of everybody," she half whispered. "He may have friends in the bar. Look, I'm going into the back room in a few minutes. Follow me there."

Raider got a drink at the bar, then took a table near the rear of the room, close to the only door that could possibly lead to the back. A few minutes later the girl walked toward the door, giving him a nervous sidelong glance as she passed by. Raider waited until she had left the barroom and closed the door after her before he made his move. He looked around. No one seemed to be paying him any special attention, so he got up and opened the door.

THE NORTHWEST RAILROAD WAR 121

The room on the other side of the door seemed to be a storeroom. Most of it was littered with boxes and barrels. It was very dimly lit, the only illumination coming from a small lamp placed on a stack of boxes.

He saw the girl immediately. She was struggling with the lock on another door on the far side of the room, a door that apparently led outside. "Marie," he called out. "Where are you going?"

She turned a frightened face back toward him. "I've... I've changed my mind," she said. "I don't want the fifty dollars."

"Wait!" he called out. "All I want to know is where I can find..."

He knew then that he'd made a big mistake. He was close to her now, and she was looking over her shoulder, her eyes wide with fear. She was looking at something behind him.

He sensed movement to his rear, and he started to spin, his right hand reaching down toward the butt of his .44, but before he could complete his turn, something hard and heavy slammed against the back of his skull. Suddenly the world exploded into a blaze of light and colors, and a moment later he felt himself falling.

CHAPTER FOURTEEN

Consciousness returned slowly to Raider. He was first aware of a terrible pain in his head. Then he was aware of other pains—a pain in his right ankle, pain in his right shoulder. And a sense of being cold.

Sight returned to him slowly, but what he saw made little sense to him, merely a rough meaningless pattern. Then he became aware that the pattern was very close, and, raising his head a few inches, he realized that he was looking down at a rough stone floor.

Suddenly he gasped as a wash of icy cold water hit him, and he raised himself up on his hands and knees. A man was standing in front of him, grinning, an empty water bucket in his hands. A voice spoke from somewhere else in the room. "If he don't sit up and start lookin' alive, give him another bucketful."

The water had done its job: Raider felt relatively awake now, and he began to struggle to a sitting position, only to find that he could not maneuver his right leg correctly. Looking back along his body, he saw that an iron chain ran from his right ankle to a ring set in stone. He was chained to the wall! A shorter chain linked his two wrists.

Nevertheless, he finally managed to sit up. The man with the bucket continued to grin down at him. Raider now looked around for the man who had spoken, and found him lounging carelessly in a chair on the far side of the room, about fifteen feet away. He was of medium size, dressed roughly, with black eyes and a shaggy black mustache. He had a long curved scar on the right side of his face. Looking more closely, Raider saw that the man was missing one finger of his left hand. Great. He'd obviously found Whiskey Joe Devlin. But not quite in the manner he'd planned.

"I've had a lot of trouble from you," Whiskey Joe said irritably.

Raider was dizzy. He shook his head, but it only made him dizzier. He waited a moment for the dizziness to pass. "A man's gotta keep busy," he finally said.

Whiskey Joe took this information glumly. "Cost me a lot of good men."

"A lot of losers," Raider retorted.

Whiskey Joe got to his feet and took a couple of steps toward Raider. "Are you a Pinkerton?" he asked.

"Could be."

Suddenly Whiskey Joe ran two steps forward and kicked Raider brutally in the ribs. Raider lost his balance and fell backwards. Whiskey Joe stepped closer and, seizing him by the hair, jerked his head erect. "I ast you a question!" he bellowed. "Are you a Pink?"

"Yep." Raider could see no harm in admitting it, and maybe a lot of harm in not doing so.

Whiskey Joe stepped back. "Well, I'll be danged. Never figured on seein' no Pinks up here in British Columbia. That Onderdonk is a little smarter than I had him pegged for."

"Yeah. A lot smarter."

Once again Whiskey Joe instantly went from calm introspection to white-hot rage. Leaping forward, he backhanded Raider twice, then spit in his face. "You got too smart a mouth, mister! Anybody ever tell you that?"

They had, of course, lots of people, but Raider was not about to bandy words with Whiskey Joe. Not chained to a wall. But if there ever came a time... Raider didn't take too kindly to people spitting in his face.

Just as quickly as he had flown into a rage, Whiskey Joe grew calm again. "How much do you people know?" he asked.

"Know about what?"

"Don't come on dumb to me. About what we been doing. All that wreckin' work on the railroad."

Raider shrugged, which made his head hurt. "Well, to tell you the truth, it's had us a little stumped. The idea of a bunch of small-timers goin' after a big outfit like the Canadian Pacific..."

Once again Whiskey Joe flew into a rage. He seized Raider by the hair, bending his neck back so that Raider was looking straight up into the man's empurpled face. "Small-timers?" he roared. "This ain't no small-time operation, buddy. We work for one hell of a big man. For a whole passel o' big men."

"Yeah, sure," Raider said doubtfully, pushing his luck a little. Fortunately, Whiskey Joe chose to prove his point rather than take it out on Raider's body. "We're in the railroad business too," he said. "On'y we're workin' for the U.S. roads, not some pissy-ass Canadian line. We don't work for no foreigners."

"Uh-huh," Raider grunted noncommittally.

Whiskey Joe started to grow angry again, but then walked quickly over to a table and snatched up a piece of paper. Returning to Raider, he stuck the piece of paper underneath his nose. "Read it, smart-ass," Whiskey Joe snarled.

Raider carefully studied the paper. It was a letter, complaining that Whiskey Joe had so far done too little to slow down the building of Onderdonk's portion of the Canadian Pacific. What Raider found most interesting about the letter was the signature at the bottom—Jay Cooke, a well-known eastern railroad magnate.

"You see?" Whiskey Joe said triumphantly. "We got us some real strong backin'. This ain't no penny-ante operation."

Raider said nothing, but privately he agreed. Jay Cooke was a powerful man, one of the richest individuals in the Unites States. And the whole thing fit. A few years earlier, when the original plans had been made in Ottawa to build the Canadian transcontinental railroad, Jay Cooke had been involved in a scandal. He'd been paying bribes to corrupt Canadian politicians in the hope of getting them to vote against the building of the road. At that time, if Canadians wanted to travel, or to ship goods between the eastern and western parts of their country, they had to do so via U.S. railroads. It was a lucrative trade. Jay Cooke had wanted to keep it that way. He, and no doubt his other fat-cat railroad tycoon friends, wanted to hold on to their monopoly, no matter what.

The trouble was, Cooke had been caught with his hands in the cookie jar. There had been a big international brouhaha, which had made Cooke, and his other corrupt friends, pull in their horns. Or so it had looked at the time. Now it was clear that Cooke had simply changed his manner of operations. To sabotage.

Raider nodded at the letter. "Yeah. We kinda had it figured that way."

"You're lyin'!" Whiskey Joe screamed. "I saw your face when you read the letter. You didn't know nothin' about it. Shit. You make me sick."

Without any warning, he kicked Raider's arm out from beneath him, so that Raider fell on his face. When he raised himself up again, he was bleeding from a cut on his cheek. "You ain't so tough now, are you, Pinkerton man?" Whiskey Joe asked, grinning.

Whiskey Joe turned and headed toward the door. "Keep a real good eye on him," he told the other man. "If he gets away, you take his place."

He turned back to face Raider, still grinning. "I'm gonna kill you, of course. But not till I feel like it. Hell, having you around is more fun than a barrel of monkeys."

Which was pretty much the way it turned out, as far as Whiskey Joe and his men were concerned. For the next three days, Raider was kept chained to his wall, and regularly abused, and not so regularly fed, and then only the worst slop. Whiskey Joe, usually in the company of two or three other men—apparently all he had left after the way Raider had decimated the ranks of his followers—continually taunted his captive Pinkerton, sometimes giving him a few more details about his connections with Cooke and the other American railroad magnates.

He tried to make it sound as if he and Cooke were buddies, drinking cronies, but Raider had little doubt that, to Cooke, Whiskey Joe was no more than an obnoxious necessity. He said this once, and Whiskey Joe beat him badly, afterward pissing on him as he lay on the hard stone floor, and as the warm stinking urine hit him, Raider vowed that if he ever got the chance, Whiskey Joe was going to regret the day he'd been born.

Raider steadily grew weaker, both from physical abuse and from lack of food and water. But he made it a point to feign more weakness than he actually felt. Finally, on the fourth day of his imprisonment, he found himself alone with his regular guard, a brutal, semi-moronic man named Sims. Sims had been particularly hard on him, and with Raider's helplessness, had come to regard the prisoner with contempt and derision. Which was what Raider was counting on now. "Sims," he called out weakly. "I've got to have some water. Feel weak...sick."

"Go fuck yourself," Sims said absentmindedly. He was seated at a table about ten feet away, playing a game of solitaire. Poorly.

"Gonna pass out," Raider muttered, swaying as he sat.

"So pass out."

"Sims...I..."

Raider collapsed, and as he fell back, his right arm

flopped out to the side, upsetting his slop bucket, so that a stinking liquid mess shot across the floor toward Sims's boots. Sims cursed and jumped to his feet. "You clumsy son of a bitch!" he snarled. "Goddamn it, I'm gonna use your face to mop up this mess!"

He strode over to Raider and bent down to haul him to his feet. Raider came up a lot easier than Sims had expected, in fact he literally leaped up, butting Sims in the face. Then he kneed him in the groin. Sims grunted and bent forward, clutching his groin, at which point Raider, clasping both hands tightly together, so that about eighteen inches of chain hung loosely in front of him, backhanded Sims across the face with the heavy piece of chain.

Sims howled and began to fall backward, which would have been disastrous for Raider because the chain that bound him to the wall wouldn't have permitted him to go after the man, but Raider reached out desperately and pulled Sims back toward him. Jamming his left hand against the front of Sims's face, low down, Raider grasped his chin while his other hand seized the back of his head. Twisting with his entire body, Raider torqued Sims's head around savagely, spinning him off his feet... but not before Sims's thick neck had broken.

Sims fell dead at Raider's feet. Raider experienced a moment of savage exultation: he'd killed one of the men who'd tormented him. However, if he didn't get loose before the others returned, he'd soon enough be just as dead as Sims, and probably after experiencing one hell of a lot of pain.

The keys to his shackles lay on the tabletop. Even pulling his chain so taut that it dug into the sores the metal had rubbed into the flesh of his ankles, he was still about eight feet short of reaching the table. If only he had something to knock the keys off the table onto the floor, where he could reach them. A stick of some kind. But there was nothing.

Except maybe his belt. But it would never reach eight feet. However, Sims had a belt too.

Raider quickly stripped off both his belt and Sims's,

then spent a couple of frustrating moments joining them. He then began to cast the heavy buckle of Sims's belt toward the table. It barely reached the keys. Once, he almost knocked the keys over the rear side of the table, which would have ended his escape attempt right there, but at last the buckle caught on one of the larger keys in the key ring, and Raider was able to drag the keys off onto the floor.

Afterward it was fairly simple to drag the key ring over to where he stood. A minute later he was free of his shackles. He immediately moved over to the far wall, where they had hung his gunbelt. The big Remington was still in its holster, and the bowie in its sheath. With weak, shaking fingers, he buckled on his weapons—and immediately felt a surge of relief. And now that he was free and armed, a killing rage almost overwhelmed him, a compelling desire to wait here until Whiskey Joe and his companions returned, and then make them pay for what they had done to him.

He had second thoughts when he inexplicably found himself lying on the floor, once again staring down at the rough stone pavement only inches from his eyes. He'd passed out and not even been aware of falling. That wasn't too good. Obviously the ordeal of the past few days had weakened him more than he'd realized. It would probably be tantamount to suicide if he stayed here to fight it out with Whiskey Joe.

So he left the house, still weak and unsteady, but able to navigate well enough to get himself onto the back of a horse he found saddled and tied up near the front of the house. Probaby Sims's mount.

He had to travel a ways before finally discovering where he was. Riding up onto a small knoll, where he had a view of the countryside, he saw that he was only a couple of miles away from New Westminster. Fifteen minutes later he was riding into the outskirts of the town.

The question was, Where to go? He had no money on him, his pockets had been cleaned out. He debated sending a wire to the agency, but suspected that the rather abrupt

THE NORTHWEST RAILROAD WAR 129

and unfriendly nature of his last message to headquarters might not exactly have left his employers in a mood to leap to his aid.

And then an image came into his mind of a tall, heavily built man with the face of one of the more benign Old Testament prophets. Judge Mathew Begbie.

New Westminster was a rather small place, so it took only a couple of inquiries to determine that Judge Begbie was in town. Raider rode directly to the house where the judge was staying, hitched his horse out front, and pounded on the door.

The door was answered by a woman who had the appearance of a domestic, probably a cook. She wrinkled her nose at the foul smell emanating from the ragged scarecrow standing at the door and attempted to shut it in his face. Raider pushed back as hard as he could. "Uh-uh. I'm not a bum. I want to talk to the judge about some criminals. Tell him... tell him that Raider wants to see him."

The expression on the woman's face made it clear that she thought Raider himself was undoubtedly a criminal of the lowest order, but she knew better than to make decisions on her own concerning the judge's work, so, after shutting the door solidly, she went upstairs to apprise her employer of the apparition at his front door.

Two minutes later, Judge Begbie himself opened the door. His usual composure failed a little when he saw Raider. "My God, man! What happened to you?"

"Had a little run-in with the men who've been sabotaging the railroad."

The judge's eyes narrowed. "Run-ins seem to be your kind of thing, and from the look of you, you came out on the losing end this time. But come in, man. You look like you're about to fall down. You can tell me about it in my study."

Raider followed the judge into a large room lined with bookcases. The judge winced openly at the smell when Raider passed close by him, so Raider was thoughtful enough to seat himself on a plain wooden chair, rather than chance ruining the upholstery on the finer pieces.

At Judge Begbie's prompting, Raider quickly recounted his capture. The judge swore softly when he heard Whiskey Joe's name. "Whiskey Joe Devlin? That's a man I'd like to get my hands on."

"Well, he ain't far away."

Raider told him where the house was. The judge immediately went to the study door and called for his housekeeper, the woman who had first answered the door. "See that Mr. Raider gets a bath," he told her. "And see that his clothes are washed. No," he amended, taking a more critical look at Raider. "See that they're burned. Fit him out with some of mine."

And then he left the house to round up help. Raider offered to go with him, but Judge Begbie convinced Raider that in his current condition he would probably be more hindrance than help. Raider didn't put up too much of a fight, and fifteen minutes later he was soaking in a big tub full of soothing hot water. He had washed and dried himself, and was dressed in some of Judge Begbie's clothes, which hung rather loosely on his wasted frame, when the judge returned. "He's flown the coop," he said disgustedly. "He must have returned not long after you escaped. He left behind the body of the dead man you told me about, but precious little else."

"So he got away."

"For now. But we'll get him in the end. He won't be able to run far enough."

Raider let his mind replay some of the things Whiskey Joe Devlin had done to him over the past few days. He could visualize the man's sneering, rage-distorted features, the long curving scar. "No, he won't," the big Pinkerton said in a low, deadly voice. "He won't be able to run far enough, even if he runs all the way to hell."

CHAPTER FIFTEEN

Raider returned to his hotel. He'd paid a couple of days ahead, but the proprietor had begun to think he was not returning. "Another day or two and I woulda sold your stuff," he said sourly.

Raider felt too beat-up to reply. He went straight to his room. His gear was still there. Digging down into his bedroll, he located his stash and restocked his pockets with money, some of which went to pay his back rent. A few more dollars went to buy himself a huge meal in the nearest restaurant. Then he returned to the hotel, warned the hotelier not to disturb him for anything, not if he valued his hide, and went to bed with the intention of sleeping for a day or so.

He was awakened by a loud knocking on his door. Groggy, sore, weak, he sat up on the narrow bed, his mood instantly foul. He saw from the light coming in through the window that it was daytime. A quick check of his watch suggested he had slept for about eighteen hours. His mouth tasted like a stagnant swamp, his body was stiff, his mind was working slowly.

More pounding on the door. "Goddamn it! Hold your water!" Raider snarled. He would have shouted, but he doubted his sleep-gummed vocal apparatus was up to the chore.

Sliding out of bed, he pulled on a pair of jeans, picked up his Remington, then, barefoot and bare-chested, walked over to the door. Standing to one side, he called out, "Who's there?"

"Pete Brody."

Pete Brody? It took Raider's still-groggy mind a moment to register the name. Of course! Pete Brody... like himself, an operative of the Pinkerton Agency. They'd sent reinforcements!

"Come on, Raider. Open up."

Raider slipped the lock on the door and swung it open. Brody, a big beefy man, filled most of the door frame. Behind him, Raider caught sight of more men. "Well, damn!" Raider said as they all pushed inside. "I guess the cavalry's finally got here."

"This is Joe, and Pat, and Henry," Brody said. The three men nodded. They were all as big as Brody. None of them smiled, not even Brody. Raider went over to where his gunbelt lay draped over a chair and shoved the Remington back into its holster before turning to face the four men again. Hot damn! With numbers like this, Whiskey Joe wouldn't stand a chance.

Except the four men were not exactly acting like allies. Joe walked over to Raider's gunbelt and lifted out his .44, which did not please Raider; he did not like others handling his weapons. He was even less pleased when Pat removed his Winchester from the corner where it was leaning against the wall. "What the hell is this?" Raider demanded of Brody.

"Now don't get excited, Raider," Brody said evenly. "We just came up here to take you back home."

"Home? What the hell do you mean, home? Miss Livonia's?"

"Uh-uh. The Chicago office."

"What? Chicago? But we'd lose too damned much time. That would give the bastard all the time in the world to disappear."

"What bastard?"

"Whiskey Joe Devlin."

"I never heard of a Whiskey Joe Devlin."

"But, then, why are you here?"

"I told you. To take you back to Chicago."

"But... Devlin. He's... Look, there's a judge here, name of Begbie. He'll tell you."

"He's the one who told us where to find you. Kinda sent us over here."

"Sent you?"

"Yeah. Asked us to bring you over to him before we left."

Raider was close to blowing up, but he forced himself to do his best to contain his anger. Obviously these men had not come here to help him. Go with them to Chicago? Not if he could help it. Except he wasn't exactly in the best position to put up much of an argument. They had his weapons, there were four of them, big bastards, and he was still weak from his captivity. However, he did have one thing going for him. They said they were taking him to see Begbie. The judge would set them straight.

Raider dressed, this time in some of his own clothes. Brody and the others picked up his gear and followed him out of the hotel. Raider expected that they would go to Begbie's house, but instead they went to a larger building, a courthouse. Begbie was waiting for them in what was obviously a courtroom, seated behind a high desk, looking every inch the judge. "Ah, you brought him," he said to Brody. "No trouble?"

"Uh-uh, Your Honor."

Judge Begbie now switched his attention to Raider. "As you know," he said, rather formally, "I have not exactly been happy about your activities in British Columbia. It's been rather insulting, an operative of a private police force, and a foreign one at that, wreaking havoc in our province. I long ago lost count of the dead bodies attributable to you. Now, I know that you, and Mr. Onderdonk, were convinced you had a reason to be here—"

"You bet I did," Raider cut in. "The sabotage on the railroad. Whiskey Joe Devlin."

"You can leave that to us now. I don't think there will be any more sabotage. I admit, we owe most of that to you, but enough is enough, Raider. We—"

"What the hell about Whiskey Joe?" Raider demanded.

The judge's manner grew distinctly icy. "From now on, Whiskey Joe is our concern. He's committed crimes in Canada. That's Canada's problem, and Canada will see that he is apprehended and punished. There is no private justice in our country, Raider. We will—"

"Sure," Raider said bitterly. "You'll take your one Mountie and—"

"More than one. The labor troubles farther down the rail line are over now. The regular contingent of Mounted Police is on its way back to British Columbia. They make up a considerable force, quite adequate to deal with Whiskey Joe Devlin."

And now a slight smile tugged at the corners of Judge Begbie's mouth. "Perhaps you haven't heard. The Mounties always get their man."

When Raider didn't react, the judge continued. "Now, as for you, Raider, I'm going to ask you . . . no, I'm going to *order* you to leave British Columbia at once. I don't like to say this, but if I see you back here in the immediate future, you will be put under arrest. Is that clear?"

He was looking sternly at Raider. Raider nodded grimly. "Yeah. Clear as water, Judge."

And it *was* clear. The presence of Pete Brody and the three men with him left little doubt in Raider's mind. The Pinkerton National Detective Agency did a great deal of work for the U.S. railroads. This work provided the agency

THE NORTHWEST RAILROAD WAR 135

with a considerable percentage of its income. Whiskey Joe had proved to Raider that he was working for one of the most powerful railroad magnates in the United States. Jay Cooke.

Cooke, alarmed at the inroads Raider was making against his saboteurs in British Columbia, must have put pressure on the head office to call off their dog. To protect their railroad revenues, the agency would have agreed to pull Raider out of British Columbia. Thus the telegram ordering him to leave, and when he refused, the dispatching of Brody and company. Yeah. It was all nice and clear.

They left that afternoon on the boat to San Francisco, Raider, Brody, Joe, Pat, and Henry, a quintet of large men, all of them armed except Raider.

From San Francisco they took the train east, sharing two compartments. There were always at least two men watching Raider. Raider groused and complained, but made a point of not causing them any real trouble. Not that he was exactly meek as a lamb; such uncharacteristic behavior would have immediately aroused Brody's suspicions.

He had a plan, of course, because he had no intention of leaving Whiskey Joe to anyone else. He wanted the man's hide nailed to a wall, and he wanted to drive in each nail personally.

He spent most of the trip resting, recovering his strength. By the time he was ready to make his break, the others were noticeably less vigilant, partly because they were now so close to Chicago.

Raider's first move was to steal his .44 back. Brody had left it in his valise, and when no one was looking, Raider removed it and slipped it into the waistband of his trousers, the butt hidden beneath his jacket.

The next move was to head for the bathroom. No one accompanied him; after all, the train was moving pretty fast, and was not due to stop until it reached Chicago in another hour.

Raider walked on past the bathroom, and then, opening the door at the end of the car, stepped through onto the outside platform. He'd ridden this train several times, and knew that it usually slowed down just before going through a small town. The small town lay just a mile or so ahead, and the train was already slowing. Raider moved down onto the lowest step, waited his chance, and finally, judging that the train had slowed enough, he jumped.

He hit running, but he was still traveling so fast his legs couldn't keep up with his body, and he fell, rolling, tucking in his arms and legs, protecting his head. When he stopped rolling, the train was past. He got up and dusted himself off.

It was only a quarter of a mile to the little town. He headed straight for the train station. He was in luck: there was an eastbound train leaving in ten minutes.

By then, Brody and the others would have discovered that he was missing. They would spend a few minutes searching the train, which would be approaching Chicago. They'd come back after him, of course, but they would assume that he had gone back west. His little surprise was that he was heading east.

He remained on the train when it reached Chicago, staying out of sight inside a compartment. There shouldn't be any trouble after that; by the time they discovered he was traveling east, he'd be in New York.

He reached his destination early the next morning. It was only a matter of an hour or so's work to discover the address of the man he was looking for. A little before noon he was walking up the steps of a big house in a fashionable neighborhood, just off lower Fifth Avenue. He pulled on the bell cord, and with commendable dispatch, a butler opened the door. "Yaaasssss," he said grandly, somewhat dubiously eyeing Raider's attire.

"I'm here to see Jay Cooke."

Another supercilious look. "Do you have an appointment?"

"Tell him it's about Whiskey Joe Devlin. Then I'll have an appointment."

The butler sniffed haughtily, then closed the door in

Raider's face. He was back rather quickly, his face reflecting a good deal more respect. "Mr. Cooke will see you now, sir."

Raider pushed past the flunky, who immediately skipped ahead of him, leading the way down a long hallway. There were signs of money everywhere: in the fine paintings on the walls, the tapestries, the costly carpets. Raider was led into a large room whose walls were lined with bookcases. A huge walnut desk was positioned against one wall. French windows led out into a garden.

The room was so cluttered with bric-a-brac, that Raider at first missed the man standing behind the desk, a short, rather portly man, with a fringe of graying hair flaring out around a mostly bald head. Luxuriant side-whiskers partially hid well-developed jowls. The man was richly dressed, with a heavy gold watch chain stretched across his brocaded vest.

"Cooke?" Raider asked.

The man's eyes narrowed. "Yes," he finally said, then he immediately came to the point. "You say you have word from Devlin?"

"Yeah. In a way."

"The idiot! I warned him that no one was ever to come here. It was all to be handled at a distance. Now give me your message and get out."

Instead, Raider turned and surveyed the room, then went over and lazily sat down in a big overstuffed armchair. Cooke bounded out from behind the desk and approached Raider angrily. "See here, you scoundrel."

"The name's Raider."

Cooke was so angry that it took a moment for the name to sink in. Then his jaw dropped open, and he stood facing Raider, gaping like a fish.

"Whiskey Joe didn't exactly send me. He did tell me a lot about you, though. You know what I mean—about you hirin' him to wreck the railroad?"

"I don't know what you're talking about."

"Oh, I think you do."

Cooke's anger was beginning to return. "I thought I had you all settled," he grated out. "I told those fools in Chicago to get you the hell out of it. Wait until I get hold of that fat idiot, William Pinkerton. He'll make you wish you had never—"

"Big Willie ain't really all that fat. Just big. An' he's only an idiot sometimes, like when he listened to you. An' when you do get hold of him, you're gonna tell him to put me back on the case. You're gonna *beg* him."

"Don't be a fool. You're finished, man. You'll be run into the farthest corner—"

"You remember a letter you sent to Whiskey Joe?" Raider asked casually.

Cooke looked confused for a few seconds, then a flash of panic showed in his eyes.

"He kept the letter," Raider said. "Kept it around to show what a big man he was. I have the letter now."

Which was a lie, but Cooke could not know that.

Cooke swallowed nervously. "What do you want from me?" he said in a low, choked voice. "Is it money? Yes, that's it, of course. How much?"

"I already told you. Ask Big Willie to put me back on the case. Tell him you'll pay whatever it costs for me to find Whiskey Joe Devlin. After all, he's a railroad wrecker, and you railroad men oughta stick together. You and Onderdonk."

"Is that all you want?"

Raider nodded, although it was not quite all that he wanted. What he really wanted was to put this fat little fraud in jail. If he had that damned letter, he'd go ahead and try, although Raider knew how little chance there was of making a rich man like Cooke pay for his crimes.

"You sound like you want Devlin pretty badly," Cooke finally said.

"Yeah, I do."

"May I just ask why?"

"Uh-uh. It's personal. You just send off a telegram to

the Chicago office. Tell 'em you want me back on the case."

Cooke was looking distinctly relieved. "I'll do better than that. I'll telephone."

Sure enough, there was a telephone box bolted to one wall, just behind Cooke's desk. "Hmmm," Raider muttered somewhat dubiously. Always suspicious of the latest technology, he had a lot more faith in good, honest, old-fashioned telegrams, but he nodded, and a few minutes later Cooke was energetically cranking the handle of his telephone. Within another few minutes he had been connected and was asking for William Pinkerton.

Raider found it somewhat confusing hearing only one side of a conversation, but Cooke seemed to be telling Big Willie what Raider had asked him to say. "I didn't fully understand what was going on up there," Cooke was explaining. "A terrible thing. Yes, your man is here now. He's explained to me... Yes. I'll put him on."

Cooke held the mouthpiece out to Raider. Raider pointed to himself, as if asking, "Who, me?" then he rather hesitantly took the receiver and moved close to the mouthpiece. "Yeah?" he grunted dubiously.

"Raider? That you?"

The tinny voice blasting into his ear made Raider jump. It was William Pinkerton's voice. Raider thought of all those miles between himself and the Chicago office, such a long ways, so he shouted his reply into the phone.

"Ow!" Pinkerton shouted back. "Don't talk so damned loud."

"Sorry." In somewhat less of a shout.

There was a moment's silence. "Raider, I don't know what kind of game you're playing, but it sounds like you're ahead on points. Get your ass back to the office and we'll talk details. Now give me Cooke."

Raider, glad to be shut of this infernal contraption, handed the receiver back to Cooke, who proceeded to wax serious. "We railroad men have to stick together," he said sternly into the mouthpiece, stealing a line from Raider. "I want that scoundrel Devlin apprehended. I'll appreciate anything you can do... Yes. Appreciative. Very appreciative."

There were a few last pleasantries, and then Cooke hung up. He looked quite pleased when he turned to face Raider. "That went well. I'm certain you will have the backing of your head office. Just as you have my backing. This Devlin fellow will be in the bag in no time."

Raider looked at the other man with some amazement. Now that he'd been cornered, Cooke seemed to have convinced himself that he'd wanted to see Whiskey Joe Devlin stopped all along. A moral cripple, like most captains of industry, a salesman to the core, Cooke had a mentality which could convince itself of anything, once the necessity became apparent.

He did have one moment of rational thought before showing Raider out. "This man Devlin," he said in a low voice. "It might be better for all if he were shot and killed, rather than simply captured."

Of course, Raider thought. So he can't tell the world who hired him in the first place.

Raider walked on out the door, never looking back, but Cooke's words followed him. "Remember," he called out, his voice quite a bit louder now. "I'll make it worth your while! You just tell me how much you want!"

CHAPTER SIXTEEN

Raider's reception in the Chicago office was rather cool. William Pinkerton himself waved him into his private office, a rather large room crammed with memorabilia, furniture, and files. William, or Big Willie as some called him, though usually not to his face, was indeed a big man, not only tall, but quite broad. Raider supposed that Jay Cooke might have a point in describing William Pinkerton as fat. He had a large moon face that sported a large mustache over a tight, down-curving mouth. His hair, heavily pomaded, was combed over the top of his skull from a part on the far left, to cover a growing bald spot.

It was his eyes, however, that most people who met William Pinkerton remembered. They were hard, piercing, relentless eyes. Eyes as relentless as the organization he headed. Desperadoes had been known to wet their pants when they looked into those icy eyes, moments before Big William's fist exploded in their face, or a bullet from his pistol tore into their body. Yes, William Pinkerton might possibly be described as fat, but Jay Cooke was the one who had been a fool when he called William Pinkerton a fool.

Pinkerton crossed his office and sat at his big rolltop desk. Raider was left standing on the large Oriental carpet that covered most of the floor. He looked around idly while Pinkerton shuffled some papers. There were some prints of hunting dogs on the wall to his right, and above the dogs, several photographs of the old man, Allan Pinkerton, the founder of the agency.

"Well, Raider," Pinkerton said abruptly. "You have a knack for landing on your feet."

Raider looked coolly down at his boss. "You don't last long at this job any other way."

It was on the tip of Pinkerton's tongue to suggest that Raider had come perilously close to losing that very job, but he thought better of it. One didn't say things like that to a man like Raider, not without the prospect of having Raider tell him just what he could do with the job. This Cooke thing wasn't worth losing an operative as good as Raider, so Pinkerton swallowed his pride. "Well, you have work to do. We've already sent out telegrams to the field offices. If this Whiskey Joe Devlin shows, we'll hear about it. In the meantime, you might like to do some research in the archives, learn more about the man."

Raider was a bit touched that crusty William Pinkerton had decided to soft-pedal his defiance of orders, his escape from the men sent to bring him back to the office, his going over the agency's head. He nodded in response to Pinkerton's suggestion, although he hated archives, hated being inside this stuffy headquarters. He figured he knew plenty about Whiskey Joe already, and he'd rather be out on the trail going after his man. But that would have to wait until he got some leads.

Accordingly, he reported to the archives and rogues gallery. Despite his initial reluctance, he soon became fascinated as he delved into the life of Whiskey Joe Devlin. There was even one faded photograph, showing Whiskey Joe in the company of a group of other men. They were as vicious-looking a bunch as Raider had ever seen. Whiskey runners. If this was the type of American Sergeant Stuart had come into contact with, no wonder he was down on the breed.

Raider spent several days familiarizing himself with Whiskey Joe's background—where he came from, where he tended to hole up when things went bad. All signs pointed to a remote corner of northwestern Montana, on the eastern slopes of the Rockies. Sure enough, when a potential sighting report came in, it was from Montana.

The Pinkerton National Detective Agency had a nationwide net of informers, people of all walks of life, who, thrilled with the idea of working with the country's premier detective agency, or perhaps interested in rewards, flooded the Chicago office with data, suspicions, suspected sightings of wanted men, and sometimes just rumors. The informants came from all walks of life: bankers, bartenders, herders, cattlemen, sheriffs, schoolteachers—the entire nation provided the agency with a finely woven net of information. The Pinkerton Agency took these reports seriously. No matter how vague, each report was analyzed, and if judged valid, inserted into the vast system of files.

The sighting concerning Whiskey Joe Devlin was convincing enough to have Raider on the road that same day, heading west via rail. The Montana area was still in the process of being opened up to railroads, and none as yet went within a hundred miles of where he was heading, so on the second day Raider left the railhead and proceeded on horseback.

The country he was riding into was very sparsely settled, a good place for a man like Whiskey Joe to hide out. It was wild country, with the Rockies lying just to the west. Raider's route took him straight toward that incredible cordillera. Hour after hour, day after day, he watched it grow in size as he approached: massive, beautiful, impassable-looking.

On the fourth day he reached the area where Whiskey Joe had been sighted, or rather, reached a town near the area. Settlements were few and far between. Checking in with his informant, a telegraph operator, he discovered that Whiskey Joe, or the man believed to be Whiskey Joe, had been spotted again, about a week ago, in a small settlement farther north, so Raider set out northward.

The route led over a narrow trail. He had only gone about a mile when he saw a man riding toward him. The man was still a couple of hundred yards away, but there was something about him...

At first Raider thought that he must be mistaken, that it couldn't be the man it seemed to be, but as they approached closer to one another, he became certain. The faded buckskin clothing had helped confuse him for a moment; the last time he'd seen this particular man, he'd been dressed in the Queen's scarlet. "My God!" he burst out. "It's Sergeant Stuart!"

And indeed it was. The Mountie pulled his horse to a stop a few feet away. His face was almost as red as the Mountie uniform Raider had last seen him wearing.

His first surprise over, Raider chuckled. "Wouldn't be doin' a little moonlightin' down here in the U. S. of A., would you, Sergeant?"

Sergeant Stuart managed to look even more embarrassed. "I didn't expect to see you in these parts."

"Why not? You know I'm after Whiskey Joe."

Sergeant Stuart's eyes immediately showed intense interest. "You have information?"

"Yep. We've had a sighting a ways north. I'm headin' up there now."

The interest remained in the Mountie's eyes. Raider's first impulse was to tell him to get the hell back to his own country tit for tat, but then he began to do some hard thinking. Whiskey Joe appeared to be heading north. That might mean that he was on his way back to Canada, and if he was heading for Canada, Sergeant Stuart might turn out to be a valuable ally. "Come on. Ride along with me," he said to the sergeant. "Two men'll do better against Whiskey Joe than one."

Surprise showed on the Mountie's face, followed by gratitude. "Thank you, Raider. You could easily have made things difficult for me... as I did for you in British Columbia."

"Ah, forget it. No hard feelin's," Raider said amiably, looking off down the trail. But privately he was thinking: Not until I figure I'm breathin' down Whiskey Joe's neck ... 'cause I want that son of a bitch all to myself.

The two men rode along for over an hour in silence, Raider stealing quick glances toward Sergeant Stuart. The Mountie was still wearing his uniform trousers and boots, but had on over them a supple buckskin shirt that reached halfway to his knees. The sleeves and collar of the shirt were hung with long buckskin fringes. That was the custom in this north country. The fringes were worn partly for decoration, but in a pinch they could be cut loose and used as leather tie strings.

A rather floppy hat sat, canted to one side, on the Mountie's head. A long blue cloth was wound and knotted around the hat's crown. At first glance the effect was rather casual, but Sergeant Douglas Stuart was not a man upon whom casualness sat well. Raider had little trouble detecting, beneath the trail clothes, the man's rigidity of purpose.

It was late in the afternoon before they reached the settlement where Whiskey Joe had been spotted. Back in Chicago, Raider had taken that old photograph of Whiskey Joe and his whiskey-runner friends and had had a larger photograph made of just Whiskey Joe's face. The man who ran the local store recognized him immediately. "Yep. He was here a couple o' weeks ago. Him and some other nasty-looking hombres bought one hell of a lot of whiskey. Real rotgut. I watched 'em doctor it up. Put in a lot of caramel coloring, sugar, a little gunpowder, and other stuff I don't wanna think about. Took off with several kegs of the stuff loaded in a wagon. Seemed to be headed north, up toward the Canadian border."

A spasm of anger passed across Sergeant Stuart's face. "He's back into whiskey running," he burst out angrily.

"That's kinda the way I figured it," the storekeeper replied.

"Then why the hell didn't you stop him? At least, why didn't you call the local law?"

The storekeeper shrugged. "Wasn't none o' my business. I didn't figure he was gonna sell that firewater to no local Indians. What he does up in Canada is between him and the Canadians."

The sergeant's face hardened. "You're definitely right on that point."

Sergeant Stuart turned and stalked away. "Hey," the storekeeper called out after him. "Who the hell are you, anyhow, asking all these questions?"

Raider, who had stayed behind, looked the storekeeper straight in the eye. "That ain't none o' your business either, pilgrim. Just like you said it ain't nobody else's business who you sell your rotgut to."

Feeling very uncomfortable staring into the hard blackness of Raider's eyes, the storekeeper swallowed rather nervously. "Well, hell, I weren't gonna say too much to the men bought that whiskey. They was one real mean-lookin' bunch."

Raider turned and followed Sergeant Stuart outside. Once he was out of sight, the storekeeper muttered, "An' there's two more real hard-lookin' bastards."

By the time Raider had mounted his horse, Sergeant Stuart was already riding north. Raider caught up to him a few minutes later. "Bothers you, don't it, this sellin' whiskey to the Indians."

"It certainly does," Sergeant Stuart said tightly. "I've seen alcohol do as much damage to the Indians as typhus, measles, or smallpox. I've seen drunken Indians sell their wives and children to get another bottle of whiskey. I've seen blood brothers kill one another in drunken frenzies. I've seen whole tribes broken apart after the whiskey runners got to them."

"That's true. Indians don't hold their liquor too well."

"It's genetic. We Europeans had thousands of years to

grow used to the effects of alcohol, to build up a tolerance. The Indian hasn't. He goes totally out of his mind when he drinks, goes crazy, thinks he's living in a spirit world—which is only natural. Thousands of years ago, say, way back when wine had just been discovered, the same thing used to happen to Europeans. Back then, particularly in the Mediterranean area, the priests and priestesses used to drink wine so that they could go into a trance and make prophecies, talk to the gods, that kind of thing. Wine began as a supernatural sacrament, a magic mind-alterer. Whiskey seems to do pretty much the same for the Indians. The trouble is, it's just too available. Wine used to be scarce as hell. Kings would hock their kingdoms for a little wine."

"I wouldn't know. Can't hardly remember back that far."

"Books . . . history. They do the remembering for you."

Raider winced. "You sound too damned much like my ex-partner."

"God forbid."

They rode on for a while before the Mountie spoke again. "We used to have lots of whiskey traders in the western part of Canada. They had regular whiskey trading posts, where they fleeced the Indians out of fortunes in skins for a few dollars' worth of whiskey. The traders built those whiskey trading posts like forts, because they found out, sometimes the hard way, that an Indian, if he had no more furs to trade, was quite likely to split the trader's skull with an ax as the easiest way to get another bottle."

"Uh-huh. I heard of one named Fort Whoopee."

"A rotten place. We closed it down a few years ago, without firing a shot. That only forced some of the traders to start wandering again, peddling their liquid death out on the trail."

"You sure don't hold much for booze, do you?"

"I told you, I've seen what it can do to the Indian."

"You talk like you like Indians."

Sergeant Stuart shrugged. "Up here in Canada, we've

always felt differently toward the Indians than you Americans. The Crown's policy was simply that it was the Indians who rightfully owned the land. Any land we used, we paid for, and until recently we didn't use much. It was the English Crown's policy to let traders handle relations with the Indians. Traders like the Hudson's Bay Company."

"Well now, that sounds real nice. Real thoughtful and generous. Course, when you take a little closer look, it ain't too hard to figure out why it worked for so long. Ice and snow, that's why. The Canadian West is hard land. Until just a few years ago, hardly anybody—white men, anyhow—wanted all that frozen ground. Not as long as the American West was still empty, and one hell of a lot easier to settle. Now, with the American West fillin' up, and the Canadian railroad bein' built, I think you're gonna see a big change."

Sergeant Stuart grimaced. "You're probably right. It's already begun. The Canadian Indian is on his way to becoming a second-class citizen inside a modern nation."

"Yep." Raider looked away from Sergeant Stuart. "I used to live with the Indians. Got to know 'em pretty well, to respect 'em, to kinda like 'em. But I always knew that they're just like any other people. There's Indians that are good people, and others that are real bastards."

Sergeant Stuart agreed. The two men rode on, intent on gaining on their quarry. If the man who'd sold the whiskey was right about the time, Whiskey Joe and his companions had a two-week head start on them. Of course, their wagonload of whiskey would slow them down considerably. The Mountie and the Pinkerton were intent on taking advantage of that fact, so they rode hard, day after day, skirting to the right of the mighty slopes of the Rockies.

They weren't really certain when they passed over the border into Canada. In the kind of country they were traveling through there were no boundary markers, but one day Sergeant Stuart remarked on the fact that they had to be in Canada. Raider waited to see if being in Canada would affect Sergeant Stuart's behavior toward him, since they were now in the Mountie's bailiwick. But Stuart, obviously a man of honor, appeared to be reciprocating Raider's acceptance of him in Montana. They continued to ride on together.

Their fifth day in Canada, they crossed over the rail line, a gleaming ribbon of steel disappearing into the distance to either side, a disturbing sight in the midst of such a wild and uninhabited place—although Raider suspected that it wouldn't stay uninhabited for long, now that modern transportation was available.

On the sixth day, they had their first real evidence that they were closing in on Whiskey Joe. Sergeant Stuart saw the man first, an Indian lying by the side of the trail, unconscious, his horse cropping grass a couple of hundred yards away. Sergeant Stuart dismounted. "Drunk," the Mountie said, rolling the Indian over. The man's greasy leather clothing was stained with vomit. An empty bottle lay a yard from his limp hand.

It took them an hour to sober the Indian up enough so that they could question him. He was surly at first, but when he discovered that Sergeant Stuart was a Mountie, he immediately became friendly. Touchingly so. "I am glad you have come," the brave said. "The Mounties' have always been the red man's friend. These men, the ones who sold me the whiskey, they took all that I had, my furs, my wife, and my horse. I stole the horse back when they were not looking, and another bottle of whiskey."

"And your wife?" Sergeant Stuart prompted.

The Indian shrugged. After all, his wife was only a woman, he could get her back later when the white men were through with her. But a horse and a bottle of whiskey, that was another matter.

The Indian gave them directions to where he had left the whiskey traders and the rest of his small band. He refused to return, saying that the traders would kill him because of the horse he had taken. Raider and Sergeant Stuart pushed on. It had been late in the afternoon when they found the drunken Indian. They were forced to make camp that night; it was far too dark to travel.

They started again at first light. It was about ten in the morning before they reached the area the Indian had described to them. Knowing what kind of men they were coming up against, Raider wanted to proceed cautiously, but Sergeant Stuart rode straight on, apparently convinced that the rightness of his mission, and the authority that had been bestowed on him by the government, was all the armor he needed.

Sergeant Stuart was about fifty yards ahead of Raider when they finally reached the encampment. Raider saw the Mountie jerk his horse to an abrupt stop at the edge of a clearing. As Raider rode forward, he noticed that Sergeant Stuart was sitting his horse motionlessly. Raider slid his rifle out of its saddle scabbard, his eyes searching the brush on either side of the trail.

Turning in the saddle, Sergeant Stuart noticed Raider's caution. "It's all right," he said dully. "The whiskey traders are no longer here. They've gone... leaving this."

Sergeant Stuart swept his arm around the clearing. Raider moved his horse up alongside the Mountie's so that he could see into the clearing. "Ah, shit," he said softly.

There were ten bodies—they counted them later— men, mostly old men, and women and children. All of them were Indians. They had been shot and hacked and mutilated. The bodies of the younger women, including any girl over eight or nine, had been stripped naked. The blood between their thighs indicated how they had been treated before being killed—for some of them, perhaps even after they had been killed.

Raider and Sergeant Stuart inspected each body, to see if anyone might still be alive. None were.

"But why?" Raider asked tightly.

Grim-lipped, Sergeant Stuart waited a moment before answering. "Who really knows? Perhaps they did it because of the man who stole his horse back. Perhaps they were molesting the little girls and their mothers or brothers protested. Perhaps they killed these people just for the fun of it. It wouldn't be the first time, not for American whiskey runners. Scum. All scum. Whatever the reason, I doubt we will ever know exactly why this was done. Perhaps not even the men who did it are sure."

They worked into the night, burying the bodies, putting them into shallow graves. When the last one had been buried, both men moved away about a mile and lay down to sleep, exhausted. Despite his fatigue, Raider at first had difficulty falling asleep. Each time he started to drift off, he was aware of a killing rage sweeping through him, a rage directed at Whiskey Joe Devlin. The man needed killing. Before, because of the treatment he'd received from Whiskey Joe when he'd been his captive, Raider had wanted to do the killing himself. He still wanted to kill the bastard, but for a wider reason now. He was convinced that it would be best if an American killed him. Maybe a way to wipe the slate clean.

When Raider finally fell asleep, he slept unusually heavily, not waking until sunlight was beating against his eyelids. He quickly sat up in his bedroll, expecting to see Sergeant Stuart still sleeping near him, but there was no sign at all of the Mountie. His gear, his horse, everything was gone. "The stupid son of a bitch!" Raider burst out.

Apparently Sergeant Stuart had decided to go after the whiskey runners all by himself.

CHAPTER SEVENTEEN

Within ten minutes Raider had broken camp and was riding after Sergeant Stuart. He pushed his horse hard, willing to take a chance on blowing the animal in his haste to catch up with the Mountie. Sergeant Stuart would probably proceed much more cautiously; after all, he was on the trail of some very dangerous men, seven or eight of them, according to the Montana storekeeper.

Raider had ridden about twenty miles when he heard the first shots. His horse was lathered and blowing badly, but he pushed the animal on. A mile farther along, the trail came out onto the top of a little rise. The ground fell away below him into a small valley; from his vantage point Raider had a fairly clear view of what was happening.

The first thing he saw was Sergeant Stuart, sitting his horse on a small knoll about four hundred yards away. Following the direction of the Mountie's gaze, Raider next saw the bandits. They were positioned in a small, half-hidden clearing about two hundred yards in front of Sergeant Stuart, a bit toward Raider's left. Because of the trees and brush surrounding their position, he couldn't see them clearly, although he suspected Sergeant Stuart could; the clearing opened out in the Mountie's direction.

A puff of smoke blossomed inside the clearing. A second later a puff of dust flew up just past Sergeant Stuart's horse.

"You men down there!" Sergeant Stuart shouted. "Stop your firing."

The Mountie's words drifted over to Raider, borne on the clear mountain air. "You're all under arrest for illegal whiskey sales and murder," Sergeant Stuart called out again. "In the name of the Crown, I order you to lay down your arms!"

Raider winced at both the nobility and the foolishness of what Sergeant Stuart was trying to do. Always the man of the law. Perhaps such an order for surrender might work with Canadians, but it sure as hell wasn't going to have much effect on American hardcases like Whiskey Joe Devlin and company.

The only reply to Sergeant Stuart's demand for surrender was a shouted curse and two more shots fired in his direction. Another puff of dust flew up near the Mountie's horse, and the horse flinched and whinnied loudly. The second bullet must have grazed or wounded it.

Raider saw Sergeant Stuart slide his rifle out of its saddle scabbard. The way he took the reins in his teeth, then raised the rifle, told Raider what he was about to do. Sergeant Douglas Stuart of the Canadian Northwest Mounted Police was about to stage a one-man cavalry charge.

"Oh, no," Raider groaned. A gallant move, but a dumb one. Raider's first instinct was to rush in from his side, attacking the whiskey runners from the flank. But from where he sat his horse there was no straight way down into that clearing. Nor could he just open fire from here; the trees around the clearing hid too many of the attackers.

But a path ran to his left, along the high ground. It looked like the path might come out behind the clearing. Raider immediately spurred his horse to the left along the path. The tired animal resisted for a moment until Raider raked his spurs against its ribs, then the horse leaped forward, stretching out into a run. Fortunately, the thick layer of pine needles on the ground muffled the sound of its hooves.

It was doubtful that anyone below would have noticed anyhow; the battle was now joined in earnest. Raider caught sight of Sergeant Stuart, standing in his stirrups, reins between his teeth, rifle held in both hands, racing forward, firing furiously. Puffs of dust from rifle shots flew up all around him, but he was making himself a difficult target, using the pressure of his knees to swerve his horse from side to side.

Raider heard one of the men in the clearing cry out. A moment later a second man stood up, screaming, holding both hands against his head, blood jetting out between his fingers.

Then the Mountie's horse was hit. The animal reared, screamed, swerved, then went down. Sergeant Stuart stood in his stirrups, throwing himself clear at the last moment, a wonderful feat of horsemanship. He tried to hit running, but he lost his footing, fell, then rolled to his feet, his rifle still in his hands, and he ran forward, still shooting.

He was within perhaps fifty yards of the whiskey runners and had just shot his third man when he was hit. The Mountie spun around as if one side of him had run into a tree limb, and he went down, his rifle spinning from his hands. A savage cry of triumph rose from the whiskey runners; two of them started forward to finish off the fallen Mountie, but by now Raider was racing his horse in amongst them from the rear.

He made no attempt to draw his rifle; the long barrel would only hinder him at such close range. With his Remington .44 revolver in his right hand and his reins in his left, he pushed his horse right into the midst of the startled men, firing rapidly.

Two men went down immediately, before they could fire a shot. Two others fired at Raider but missed because

THE NORTHWEST RAILROAD WAR   155

they flinched away as his horse thundered toward them. Raider didn't miss; he fired twice more, the heavy slugs taking one man in the throat, the other low in the rib cage.

There appeared to be only one man left on his feet. Reacting more quickly than the others, he had run back toward the cover of the trees, where the horses were. Raider whirled his mount, bringing the animal around so violently that it nearly fell. He cursed the screaming, half-maddened animal; he was eager to race after the man, because he had recognized him—it was Whiskey Joe Devlin.

Whiskey Joe scrambled up into the saddle, firing at Raider as he swung his mount away. Raider fired back, cursing when he realized he'd just expended his last bullet. He shoved his pistol back into its holster and was reaching down for his rifle when his horse suddenly screamed, shuddered, then reared high. As the animal went down, Raider caught a glimpse of one of the men he'd shot, propped painfully up on one elbow, a pistol in his hand. He'd just shot Raider's horse.

Raider twisted free of the animal as it fell, fighting to keep from being pinned beneath its weight. He hit hard, the force of the blow partially stunning him, then he rolled to one side as the man who'd shot his horse fired again, the bullet tearing at the sleeve of Raider's jacket. The big Pinkerton's hand slapped at his pistol butt, then he remembered that the .44 was empty. And his rifle was back with the dead horse.

Abandoning the pistol, he reached toward the back of his belt for his bowie, jerked the huge knife free, then drew his hand back, ready to throw the bowie. But now he wished he'd scrambled after the rifle, because the wounded man had drawn a bead on him and was about to fire. Standing there with his arm pulled back, Raider knew he made a wonderful target, but he threw anyhow, hoping to kill the man even if the man's bullet killed him.

A bullet smacked into the man's side a second before the bowie knife slammed into his chest. It was the bullet in the side that ruined the man's last shot—that bullet zinging by Raider's ear—but it was the knife that killed him.

Raider quickly looked to his right. Sergeant Stuart, about fifty yards away, was propped up on his elbows, his smoking rifle thrust out ahead of him. It was his shot that had spoiled the man's aim. And then Sergeant Stuart collapsed on top of his rifle.

Raider's first instinct was to run to the wounded Mountie, but battle-craft made him check his enemies first. They were all dead, six of them. As for Whiskey Joe Devlin, Raider could hear the thud of his horse's hooves fading away in the distance.

Raider reloaded his pistol as he headed for Sergeant Stuart. Kneeling beside the wounded Mountie, he at first thought he was dead: there was a lot of blood. Then Sergeant Stuart groaned and tried to raise himself up on his elbows again. "Take it easy," Raider said. "You got him. They're all dead."

"Whiskey Joe too?" the Mountie asked in a weak but impassioned voice.

"Uh-uh. He got away."

The Mountie struggled up a little higher. "Get him! Go after him!" he begged, then flopped down again.

"Hey, take it easy," Raider insisted. "First we gotta see how bad you're hit."

"You're wasting time," Sergeant Stuart gasped. He appeared to be weakening quickly. "Get . . . him."

"Goddamn it, shut up!" Raider snapped. He carefully rolled the Mountie over. The right side of his buckskin shirt was soaked in blood. The bullet that had brought him down had drilled a hole into the leather. Raider almost missed the actual wound; it was lost amidst the steadily welling blood. He ran back to the man he and Sergeant Stuart had killed, jerked the bowie out of his chest, then ran back to the Mountie and used the knife to cut away his coat and shirt.

The bullet had gone in low on the right shoulder. Probably too high to hit the lung, Raider decided. There was no exit wound, so the bullet was still inside. Probably real deep. He'd have to get the Mountie to a doctor or he'd die.

Transportation wasn't going to be easy. Raider's horse was dead, and so was Sergeant Stuart's. Whiskey Joe had taken one horse and driven off the rest. Raider bandaged Sergeant Stuart's wound as best he could, then spent the next half hour tracking down one of the loose mounts and coaxing it back to the clearing. He removed the equipment from his own dead horse and transferred it to the captured animal. That left them with only one horse, which wasn't as bad as it sounded, since Sergeant Stuart wasn't in any condition to ride.

So Raider set about building a travois to carry the wounded man. First he cut two long alder poles, notched them, then attached flexible cross-members made of willow. He laid the Mountie's bedroll on top of the travois, then attached the upper end of the two alder poles behind his horse's saddle.

Sergeant Stuart passed out while Raider maneuvered him onto the travois, which was all right with Raider; he was getting tired of the Mountie's constant, half-whispered demands that he abandon him here and ride on alone after Whiskey Joe.

They set out a little after midday. It was slow going, with Raider riding the horse part of the time but at other times dismounting to help the drag end of the travois over particularly rough stretches. Sergeant Stuart regained consciousness from time to time, and each time Raider reassured him that they were heading in the direction Whiskey Joe had taken, which was true, not because Raider was presently concentrating on catching up with Whiskey Joe, but because that was the direction in which the nearest settlement lay, maybe two days ahead.

The settlement actually turned out to be a small town, including a resident sawbones. The doctor looked a little shaky at first, probably not yet having started his daily drinking, but he steadied down just fine as soon as he started cutting the bullet out of Sergeant Stuart.

When the operation was over, with Sergeant Stuart out

like a light from the pain, and from the whiskey the doctor had poured down him as a painkiller, Raider set out to see what he could discover about the present whereabouts of Whiskey Joe. Being such a small place, it wasn't difficult to learn that Whiskey Joe had passed through two days before, after buying himself a fresh horse and plenty of trail supplies.

Raider figured the horse he had would do, but he bought some supplies. He made camp that night just outside town. The next morning he almost rode out directly, but finally decided to drop in on Sergeant Stuart.

The Mountie was awake, and not looking too bad, considering how he'd looked the day before. "You're going after him, then?" he asked Raider.

When Raider nodded, the Mountie jerked his chin to the side. "It'd probably help a lot if you took Gaston with you. Few men know this northern country as well as he does."

Raider had been aware of another man standing by the far wall, and now he turned to face him. He was short and stocky, with a face weathered dark by a lifetime of outdoor living. He was dressed in a motley but serviceable-looking collection of buckskin, leather, sashes, and beads. A battered fur hat sat rakishly on his head. His lower legs and feet were encased in a bewildering combination of leggings, moccasins, and mukluks. His only apparent armament consisted of a long skinning knife, worn at the left side of his belt.

Sergeant Stuart waved the man over. "Raider, this is Gaston Paradis. He's one hell of a scout and woodsman. Take him along, and I guarantee you'll make much better time."

It was on the tip of Raider's tongue to refuse the offer; he usually preferred working alone. It was Gaston Paradis's eyes that changed his mind, or perhaps the man's entire face. It was one of the happiest faces Raider had ever seen—happy, clever, tough, and shrewd, all at the same time. Here was a man who both loved life and knew how to live it. "That okay with you, Gaston?" he asked.

Gaston's face split into a huge grin. "By gar, it sound like fun. There ees nothing I like better than to chase down some badman for the Mounties. Even more fun than hunting grizzly bears."

Raider looked questioningly at Sergeant Stuart. "He means it," the Mountie said weakly. He was looking tired again. "When I've had a little rest, I'll follow along."

"Yeah. Sure."

Sergeant Stuart looked at Raider with no little irritation. "I won't be long behind," he insisted.

"Whatever you say," Raider replied. Then he turned to Gaston. "Let's go get your bear," he said.

Gaston grinned again. "Sure. An' maybe we take his scalp, huh?"

Looking into the little man's eyes, Raider suspected that he meant it. He had a feeling, then, that with Gaston Paradis on his trail, Whiskey Joe Devlin was in the biggest trouble of his life.

CHAPTER EIGHTEEN

Raider and Gaston rode out that afternoon. Raider noticed that Gaston looked far from comfortable on a horse.

"Like better walkin'," Gaston replied tersely when Raider asked.

Gaston Paradis was a Métis. Métis was the French-Canadian way of saying half-breed, Gaston being half French, half Cree Indian. He was a loquacious man, when the situation called for being loquacious, and very quiet when it was time to be quiet.

Raider estimated Gaston to be about fifty years old. He was surprised when Gaston told him he was sixty, at least, as far as Gaston knew, the date of the Métis's birth being a bit vague in his mind.

"All my life, a free man," Gaston said proudly. "Hunter, trapper, voyageur. For almost fifty year I travel over this big land. I travel up and down the rivers in the old days, when the company send us for the furs. Almost freeze my ass to death maybe a hunderd time. Had ten wives, all good Indian girls."

THE NORTHWEST RAILROAD WAR   161

Raider flinched. To him, even one wife seemed far too many. But ten? Of course, he was aware of the habit, along the far frontier, of white men taking an Indian girl for a "wife." The girls were simply bought, usually by giving her father a bottle of whiskey or an old rifle, or perhaps a length of cloth. Raider had known some girls to come along with their new husbands willingly, eager for some adventure, or simply for the sex. Others had to be dragged, and at the first opportunity ran back to their tribal home. Sometimes the girl's father beat or even killed the girl, especially if the white man came to him and demanded the return of the goods he had given for her. In the tribes, a woman was usually the property of some man—either her father or brothers or husband.

When a white man—a trapper, a voyageur, or a trader —moved on, he often abandoned his Indian wife, along with any children he'd had by her, although sometimes such a strong bond grew up between the two that the white man spent the rest of his life with his squaw. Gaston had been the result of one such union, which, because of his frontier life, had given him certain advantages. He was white enough to move into at least the fringes of the white world, and his tribal connections through his mother gave him an entry into the world of the Indian.

As they rode along, Gaston regaled Raider with tales of the old days, when huge fleets of *bateaux,* the large wooden sailing vessels of the fur traders—enormous canoes, actually—set out from the East each spring on the summer-long voyage up the rivers into the far Northwest, returning in the fall with immense loads of skins and furs. "Those were good times!" Gaston said forcefully. "The only life for Gaston Paradis is the life of the voyageur."

Raider had always considered himself a considerable woodsman and scout, but he was awed by Gaston's understanding of the land they were traveling through. Gaston lived and breathed his surroundings; there seemed to be nothing he did not notice. When Raider took him back to the place where he had last seen Whiskey Joe, neither of them had any trouble picking up the fugitive's tracks, but later, when Raider knew that he would have lost the trail for sure, Gaston was able to follow effortlessly, whether it was through swamps, forests, or over hardpan.

However, Whiskey Joe had a considerable lead over them, and he seemed to be holding it. "This one, he know the woods pretty damn well," Gaston said with grudging admiration when they had come to a point in the pursuit where Whiskey Joe had used some trail tricks to try to lose any pursuers. Raider and Gaston were able to follow well enough, but each problem along the trail slowed them down more than they could afford.

The day finally arrived when they could no longer follow Whiskey Joe on horseback. On the fifth day, the Pinkerton and the scout reached a small settlement on the shores of the Athabasca River. Here they found Whiskey Joe's horse: he had traded it for passage down the river on a boat. No other boats were due to leave for several days.

Raider was intensely disappointed, but Gaston was delighted. "Good. Now we get rid of these damn horses."

Gaston made a deal with the locals to trade the horses for a birchbark canoe, some supplies, and a little money. It was here that Gaston insisted that Raider purchase a heavy fur coat. "Gonna get cold soon. Real cold. You try to travel 'ere in what you got, your ass is gonna freeze solid."

It was now late August, and, while there was a nip in the air some mornings, Raider found the weather quite tolerable. Eyeing the heavy fur distastefully, he said as much to Gaston.

"Hah! You just wait a little while. Up 'ere in this north country, we 'ave only three different season—July, August, and winter!"

So the heavy fur and the other supplies went into the bottom of the canoe. The canoe itself was quite a marvelous piece of work: light, watertight, and strong. They set off immediately, both men paddling rhythmically, and with the current helping them they made good time. Much better time than they could have made on horseback.

Now Gaston was totally in his element. Raider was a strong man, and accustomed to hard work, but the little Métis never seemed to tire. Each day they paddled as long as there was daylight, making camp along the riverbank at night. Several times, when there were rapids, they had to portage the canoe around the obstruction, and then the craft's lightness proved its utility. Sometimes, when the ground they had to travel over was particularly rough, they had to carry the canoe separately, then go back for their equipment, which slowed their progress. Fortunately, Whiskey Joe was undoubtedly experiencing the same delays.

In less than a week they reached Lake Athabasca. Here, inquiries indicated that Whiskey Joe had continued on north, perhaps hoping that if he was able to lose himself in country wild enough, any pursuit would dwindle away.

So they paddled across the lake, which took them the better part of a day. The next day they entered the Slave River, and now the journey became much more difficult. The Slave was a twisting and treacherous stream, and the portages became more numerous. On one occasion they were not quick enough, and the canoe was damaged on some rocks. They lost two days while Gaston hunted through the forest along the riverbank for the right materials, then laboriously patched the canoe.

The country was becoming wilder, more desolate. They were now in the taiga, the true north country, an immense flat area sparsely covered by a scattered forest of conifers. August had given way to September, and it was truly becoming cold now; some mornings there was a thin skin of ice on shallow puddles.

Raider noticed that Gaston was becoming somewhat nervous. Finally, he asked if anything was wrong.

Gaston hesitated before answering. "Maybe just habit," the old voyageur finally said. "For so many years, traveling this country, bringing home the furs, when this time of year come, by gar, if you were not heading back home, you would not get home. The rivers freeze up, and they are our highways. Frozen rivers, no boats move."

After a few days of paddling up the Slave, they finally reached Great Slave Lake, an immense body of water bordered by seemingly endless wilderness. Raider, never a man comfortable with cities and civilization, was feeling the immensity of this wild land seeping into him. Maybe Gaston was right. Maybe, living in and off of this land, Gaston had indeed had the happiest of all possible lives, a man living as men were meant to live.

They spent another three days coasting along the southern shore of the lake, finally reaching Fort Providence inside the mouth of the Mackenzie River. Fort Providence was, and had always been, essentially a trading post, one of the old outposts of empire, the means the British had used to control this country. Rather than appointing governors, soldiers, and bureaucrats to administer this vast wild area, they had simply granted a charter to a commercial firm, the Hudson's Bay Company, giving the company's directors the right to all commercial ventures within their vast franchise—as long as it did not unsettle the Indians' way of life.

It did, of course, to some extent change that way of life, since the Indians soon became dependent on the wonderful artifacts the white traders brought: steel knives, metal cooking pots, steel sewing needles—and of course, firearms. For several generations the Indians had had something to trade for these marvelous commodities, something of which they had more than they could use. Furs. Millions of furs, until, as the years passed, the heavy trapping necessary to accumulate all those wonderful artifacts had nearly wiped out the beaver, the fox, the marten, and most of the other fur-bearers.

At Fort Providence, Raider and Gaston discovered that Whiskey Joe was still keeping ahead of them. He had taken the steamboat up the Mackenzie River.

"Hah! You have him now!" Gaston declared jubilantly. "This time of year, going up the Mackenzie is a one-way trip."

The Mackenzie, as it turned out, was a mighty waterway that ran all the way up to the Arctic Ocean. Whiskey Joe must have believed that his trail had been lost long ago. Perhaps he intended to hole up in an essentially unreachable area until springtime, when the crimes of Whiskey Joe Devlin would be old news.

The hell with that, Raider decided. He'd go after the bastard, even if the chase took him all the way to the North Pole. It was hard to forget those murdered Indians, not to mention his own spell of unpleasantness with Devlin. The trouble was, he was going to have to go it alone; Gaston refused to go any farther.

"You see, I have a wife, a family," the little voyageur told him rather sheepishly. "If I do not go back now, while the rivers still run, it will not be easy to return to them before next spring. Maybe you should do the same thing—go back to where it is warm, then return to find your man when the waters move again."

Raider refused. He was determined to go on.

Gaston shook his head dubiously. "You do not know the far north. In winter, it is not easy to survive."

He did not even have faith in Raider's new fur coat. "You need special things up there. And you have to know how to use them."

Finally accepting Raider's sense of purpose, Gaston shook the big man's hand, then shoved off in the canoe for the trip south. Raider watched him paddle away until the little speck that was man and canoe was lost against the dark green of the forest. Then he boarded the steamboat, feeling lucky that he was able to do so. It was the last steamboat of the year. The one before had been meant to be the last, which had probably influenced Whiskey Joe's decision to take it, but the captain of this boat, believing that he could make the round-trip before the river froze over, and knowing the big profit he would make if he succeeded, was willing to gamble.

The journey north up the Mackenzie was smooth but awesome. Raider was now passing through the tundra, an enormous waste of muskeg and swamp, covered by not much more than scattered grasses and a few low bushes and mosses. Within another few weeks this entire area would be a waste of white, the muskeg frozen several feet deep.

Raider soon found that the vastness and emptiness of the land was working a subtle change in him. With so much aloneness out there, he himself, each man in fact, seemed to take on a uniqueness that was almost... godlike.

The journey, with the captain pouring on the steam to the point of rashness, was relatively short, only a little over a week. By the time they were nearing the end, the boat found itself pushing on through a thin skin of river ice each morning. They finally arrived at a small place called Inuvik, where the captain had the boat unloaded with feverish haste.

"Are you really sure you don't want to travel back with us?" he asked Raider somewhat nervously. "I sure as hell don't like leaving passengers up here this time of year."

But Raider insisted on pushing on. The word was that another white man had come through this way two weeks earlier, heading north toward an Eskimo village called Tuktoyaktuk. Raider had purchased a horse back at Great Slave Lake, and he now saddled the animal and lashed his equipment behind the saddle.

"You shouldn't oughta do that," the captain warned him. "This ain't no kinda horse country."

But Raider was adamant. He knew from reports that Whiskey Joe was afoot, and he figured that being mounted would give him the edge. Besides, he'd been a mounted man ever since he was a boy, and like most mounted men, had always felt a certain measure of condescension, approaching contempt, toward those who walked. That had been one of the hardest parts about his journey with Gaston—the lack of a horse. Being used to riding, his muscles didn't take kindly to hoofing it. The early portages had left him aching in every muscle from the waist down. Gaston had soon talked him into changing his riding boots for moccasins, but now he was in boots again, on a strong animal, with the end of the chase in sight. Whiskey Joe, on foot, was as good as caught.

It might have worked... if the weather had held. Actually, the first day of travel suffered from the unseasonable warmness of the weather—the muskeg was still soft, and the hooves of Raider's mount sank in deeply, slowing the animal so much that Raider often had to dismount and lead it.

Then on the third day the temperature abruptly dropped, freezing the muskeg almost overnight. Now riding was easier, the thick crust of ice bearing the horse quite well. Raider figured that now he would be able to reach Tuktoyaktuk by the end of the day. Whiskey Joe could not be far away.

About ten that morning, the storm hit, the first full storm of the winter. Raider had noticed that it was getting incredibly cold; there was a layer of frozen mist close to the ground, keeping him from seeing exactly where his horse was putting its hooves. Next, a terrible wind blew up, blasting into Raider's face. He pulled the collar of the fur coat around the lower part of his face, then tied his hat on by lashing a bandanna over the hat's crown, then under his chin.

It began to snow. Within an hour Raider found himself at the center of a world of unrelieved white, able to see only a few feet. He'd been in cold country before, had traveled through the Rockies and over the plains in what he had once believed to be terrible weather, but now those memories seemed to be tropical in comparison to what he was currently experiencing. Before, snow had meant to him that it might get a little warmer, but not here. The temperature still seemed to be dropping alarmingly. Raider had no way of knowing it, but before the storm was over the temperature would drop in some areas to as low as eighty degrees below zero.

He found it difficult to continue on, and knew that both

he and his horse were in danger of freezing to death. He had to find shelter and find it fast.

But there appeared to be nothing out there, only the muskeg, nothing high enough to protect him and his mount from that terrible wind. There wasn't even enough snow as yet to build himself a snow shelter.

Raider felt his strength waning. The cold was an agony, his body a pain-wracked frozen lump. Soon his horse could not carry him any longer, and Raider slipped to the ground. He stumbled, because he could feel nothing below his knees, but, leaning a little on his horse, he staggered along.

And then the wind began to diminish, dying away within minutes. Raider expected to hear a wonderful silence after that terrible demonic screaming, but instead another noise intruded on his consciousness: a deep, pervading, growling, cracking sound.

And then the white mist lifted and Raider found himself staring at a horrifying sight. Just a few hundred yards ahead the world reared up, white, and jagged, and moving, a shifting wall of ice, cracking apart, reforming, rising, falling, all to the accompaniment of the most terrible sounds.

He had reached the Beaufort Sea. The vast expanse of the pack ice lay before him, driven against the land by the force of the wind.

Raider was only vaguely aware of what he was looking at. A terrible lassitude was sweeping over him, held at bay only by the pain in those parts of his body that had not yet grown numb from the cold.

He was aware of his horse going down; the animal was no longer capable of continuing. Raider felt himself going down too, and knew that he had reached the end of his trail. He'd made the mistake of not taking seriously enough the land he was traveling through. In the wilderness, that kind of mistake was usually the final mistake.

Raider huddled next to his dying horse; somehow there seemed to be very little heat coming from the animal's body. He looked around desperately for something else to shelter behind, because the wind was rising. That terrible white mist was starting to blow around him again, obscuring the pack ice, although he could still hear its terrible voice.

As he was sliding into a final unconsciousness, Raider was vaguely aware of something moving. Something large and white and furry. A bear? A damned polar bear?

Maybe two of them. God! What now? Was he going to end up as a pile of bear shit?

Then . . . blackness.

CHAPTER NINETEEN

He vaguely remembered blood, blood all around him, huge amounts of it, hot and sticky, giving off an oddly metallic smell.

The memory flooded through Raider's mind, as the blood had flooded around him, warm, slick, and then he became aware of another kind of warmth, a softness, accompanied by a rank but comforting smell. For a moment the image of the blood faded from his mind, replaced by memories of Madame Livonia's. He could swear he felt a woman's breasts pressed against his side, felt the length of her naked body next to his.

He abruptly opened his eyes and twisted his head to the right. The light was dim, but he found himself looking into a flat, broad-nosed female face, a face that was smiling encouragingly at him.

His eyes darted away. He was inside some sort of structure, lying next to a woman, beneath a pile of furs. He was naked. So was she. He could feel her warm skin against his.

There was movement a few feet away. His eyes jerked in that direction. He saw two half-naked men, with faces as flat as the woman's, sitting on top of a pile of skins, watching him. The moment he saw their faces, memories of the blood returned with stunning force.

The two Inuit (the Eskimos' name for themselves) who found Raider—they were the large white furry shapes that had appeared out of the storm—knew that they'd have to act fast if this already half-frozen stranger was not to die. They had been on their way back to their house when they had noticed a large lump on the ground ahead of them, quickly being buried under snow, which was now falling much more thickly, driven in blinding swirls by the wind. Investigating, they had discovered a dead horse and a nearly dead man.

Their reaction was quick and efficient. In a land this harsh, with man constantly pitted against the elements, it was only normal that a human life be considered valuable. Even a stranger's life. What was most important was to halt the quick freezing that had begun to take over the stranger's body as his energy waned.

A quick examination indicated that the horse had only recently died; there was still a residual warmth detectable on its skin. One of the men pulled out a knife and quickly sliced open the animal's belly. Clouds of steam rose into the frozen air as the animal's guts were exposed. The men quickly stuffed Raider into the cavity, enfolding the horse's hot, steaming innards around him. That was the blood Raider remembered. And the initial warmth, which had halted his rapid slide into hypothermia.

One man had gone back to their dwelling to fetch a sled. When he'd returned, Raider was beginning to freeze again; the horse's body was cooling fast. They got him back to the house as quickly as they could, hauled him inside, where it was warm, and, after stripping him naked, stuffed him beneath a pile of furs. They had stuffed the naked girl in after him, knowing there are not many things in the world as likely to raise a man's body temperature as the warm, soft body of a naked girl.

Which is the scene Raider woke up to: the warm female flesh, the feeling of warmth, the dim light inside the Inuit house, the two men looking at him, his own nakedness.

His first reaction involved a moment of panic. Somehow he'd ended up in bed with someone's wife or daughter and had been caught in the act. Not an unusual situation for Raider. Automatically, his hands scrabbled around beneath the furs, looking for a weapon with which to defend himself, but his groping fingers found only the soft warm inside of the girl's thigh.

She giggled and moved a little closer, smiling invitingly into his face. Raider glanced over at the two men. For some reason they were smiling too. Then, realizing that this stranger must be oddly shy, they politely turned their backs and moved to the far side of the building's single room.

The girl, not giggling now, indeed, looking rather purposeful, snuggled closer to Raider, moving her body in a slow undulation that had unmistakable overtones. She rubbed her nose against his, and with her so close, he again became aware of the rather rancid odor. The girl, Inuit-style, had rubbed whale blubber into her skin—several days ago. The rancid blubber stank.

Not that Raider was paying much attention to the smell. Having recently survived what had seemed at the time to be certain death, he now felt incredibly alive. And horny. Despite a certain amount of residual weakness, he felt his body stirring in response to the girl's increasingly energetic movements, particularly when she opened her thighs and draped one leg over his body, rubbing her groin against the side of his leg. Raider was aware of heat and moisture and softness. Of firm breasts pressed against his right side. Of the girl's hot breath against his neck.

The rest was instinct. Within another few seconds he was ready, and the girl swung on top of him, straddling his body, pressing down until she had engulfed him, and for the next few minutes the terrible cold and the terminal bleakness of the place where he had almost died became only a memory. He lost himself in the warmth, the pleasure, the sight of the girl working above him, her face glowing with sensuality, her almond eyes staring off into space, her breasts jiggling in the most marvelous manner as her movements became increasingly wild and insistent.

When it was over, Raider glanced in the direction of the men. One of them turned and grinned at him. The girl, sliding rather wetly off his body, slipped out from beneath the skins and went over to sit beside the one who had grinned. He laughed, and playfully slapped her naked buttocks. She laughed too, although a bit shakily, still partially in the grip of her earlier passion, then she pressed herself more tightly against the man's side. When he put one arm around the girl's waist and gave her an affectionate squeeze, Raider realized that the man was probably her husband or lover. Yet he'd just watched her make love to a stranger. Curioser and curioser. Raider was beginning to wonder if maybe he'd died after all and gone to Heaven. Then he thought of the rancid blubber smell. Uh-uh. This wasn't Heaven, this was real, but for the time being it would do. Tired of worrying, Raider rolled over inside his warm cocoon of skins and fell asleep.

Thus began a rather interesting portion of Raider's life. He stayed with the Inuit for over a month. There was not much choice: the incredible cold outside the little house made traveling a chore. There was plenty of company. On his second day there, more Inuit arrived, three women and two men, ranging in age from a girl probably about fifteen years old to a man who looked like he might be in his sixties. They all lived communally in the house, being, as Raider later found out, members of an extended family.

The house itself was ingeniously designed to protect its inhabitants against the terrible Arctic winter. The main part of it was shaped more or less like an irregular and somewhat flattened and elongated dome, about thirty feet across, constructed of pieces of flat fieldstone and turf. The entrance was a long low tunnel, to keep the living quarters as far from the outside air as possible. Inside, the Inuit lived on a raised shelf toward the rear of the building. The lower portion was a storage area, where food was kept, and was so cold that everything left there soon froze solid.

The living shelf was amazingly warm, so warm that at first Raider had looked around for a roaring fire, but the source of the heat was a small whale-oil lamp, set just below the living shelf. At the rear of the shelf was a tiny air exhaust vent, a narrow slit between stones, that created a very slow draft. Frigid air entered via the tunnel entrance, passed very slowly over the oil lamp, then, being heated, rose up into the living area, eventually being exhausted through the rearward air slit. A masterpiece of survival engineering.

The heating system worked almost too well. To Raider, it was damned hot up on that platform, probably in the middle eighties. As a result, most of the house's inhabitants went naked, or nearly so. All in all, it was a cozy scene.

Raider soon discovered that his experience with the girl was not an isolated example of the physical freedom that prevailed among these people. Winter was long and boring, fellow human beings few and far between. In the boredom of the long winter nights, the Inuit turned to fun and games. There was one game in particular that at first embarrassed Raider, but he soon got into the swing of it. The game went this way: with everyone, male and female, sitting or lying about in various stages of nudity, some wag would blow out the light, and in the ensuing total darkness, a hilarious sexual game would follow, each person reaching out for the nearest body, not sure in the dark just who it might be. It was a game of sounds, at first pleased female giggles and low male laughter, the sounds gradually changing into eager panting and lusty moans. Raider became an enthusiastic player of this particular game. Within the first two weeks, he was relatively certain that he'd made love to every female in the place.

From time to time other Inuit would drop by, usually men who had been off on a hunt and were looking for warmth and human companionship for the night. More then once a husband signaled to his woman that he would not mind if she were to entertain the stranger. The women usually responded eagerly. In such tiny societies, part of the reason for such behavior was, of course, due to an instinctive hunger for new blood to enrich their genetic line. Raider, as a true outsider, a man of another race, was in particular demand among the women, and once he'd gotten beyond the smell of the rancid blubber that the women smeared onto their bodies to soften their skins, he was quite willing to help found whole new races of people.

Despite the pleasantness of his present experiences, and his relief at having been saved from freezing, Raider never lost sight of the reason he'd come to this frozen land. Whiskey Joe Devlin. He tried to discover if another white man had been seen in the area, but at first got nowhere. Nobody spoke English, and Raider sure as hell didn't speak Inuit, so he just rode with his current run of luck and set about learning as much as he could about survival in the far frozen north.

His first imperative was clothing. Obviously, his boots and trousers and even that rather clumsy fur coat were not going to insure his existence against such terrible cold. His hosts set about fashioning him some local clothing: sealhide trousers with the fur side in; warm, waterproof mukluks for his feet; a skin shirt, the leather softened by the teeth of the women; and most importantly, a knee-length parka with a wolf's-fur hood that peaked so far out in front of his face that little body heat was lost.

Raider had unknowingly paid in advance for his new clothing by providing the Inuit with a windfall of free meat—his horse. For two weeks they lived off the unfortunate animal. The horse had been cut up and dragged back to the house. Pieces of it lay below in the cold storage area, frozen solid, ready for chunks to be hacked off for each night's stew.

When he had been outfitted with his new clothes, Raider joined the men in their hunting forays. He got used to standing motionless next to a seal's blow hole, waiting for it to surface for air. The moment the seal's head broke the surface, one of the hunters would strike with his long harpoon, slamming the barbed bone tip into the seal's thick neck. The harpoon head would come loose from the shaft and the wounded animal would immediately dive back below the ice, but it was now fastened to its hunters, up on the ice, by the long hide line fastened to the harpoon head. Usually the seal would eventually die, and they would haul its body to the surface. Sometimes they would lose seal, harpoon, and most of the line. Grave losses, in a land where every artifact was hard to come by.

Raider had been with the Inuit for about a month when a hunter finally came by who spoke a little English. It was a difficult and frustrating conversation, but Raider finally elicited the information that there was indeed another white man about twenty miles to the east, living with another group of Inuit.

The hunter tried to explain to Raider that this other white man was not a good man. "He make people feel . . . how I say?"

The hunter finally got his point across by pantomiming nervousness. From the description, Raider was pretty sure that the hunter must be describing Whiskey Joe, a son of a bitch capable of making most good people feel nervous.

Apparently the Inuit were too hospitable to throw this unpleasant white man out into certain death, although the hunter indicated to Raider that they were getting close to that point. Only twenty miles away? Maybe he finally had the bastard.

Raider was making plans to cover those twenty miles when, a couple of days later, another hunter who spoke a little English reported that another white man had been seen off toward the west. That created a problem. Which one should he check out first?

The next day, Raider was sitting just about naked on a pile of skins, mulling over this latest information, when the din of an arriving dog team filtered in through the entranceway. Raider was struggling into his seal-hide trousers when a man came scrambling in through the entrance tunnel. Although the man was a mass of furs, there were enough white-man features to warn Raider that this was no Inuit. He immediately groped for his .44.

"Hold on! Put down the gun," a familiar voice called out from way back in its wolfskin parka hood.

"Jesus! Sergeant! How the hell did you get here?" Raider demanded.

Sergeant Stuart pushed back the hood of his parka. "The hard way."

The Mountie climbed up onto the living step and began taking off his parka. His eyes ran up and down Raider's nearly naked frame. "Gone native, I see."

Raider flushed. "Better'n freezin' to death. One hell of a lot better. These are good people. Been real nice to me."

Sergeant Stuart glanced over toward one of the women, who, breasts bare, was smiling back at him invitingly. "I'll bet," the Mountie said, something approaching a smile slowly stealing over his severe features.

"Okay. Enough dirty stories," Raider replied, grinning back. "Now tell me what's been going on."

The sergeant continued to strip off most of his clothing, leaving only his skin trousers. Sitting next to Raider, he began his story. "I left the doctor's a couple of weeks after you did, following your trail. I got as far as Great Slave Lake and found out you'd gone on north. The last boat had left, so I got hold of a canoe and a couple of strong paddlers and headed up the Mackenzie after you, until the ice was too thick to go on. By then I was close to a Mounted Police post and was able to abandon the canoe and outfit myself with a dog team. It was a long hard haul, but I got through. Now, where's Devlin?"

Right to the point. "I think he might be about twenty miles from here. I was figurin' on goin' after him."

Sergeant Stuart nodded gravely. "Good. But now we can *both* go."

CHAPTER TWENTY

They set out the next morning, Sergeant Stuart, Raider, and three of the Inuit men, including the visiting hunter who spoke a little English. They were using Sergeant Stuart's dog sled, which considerably speeded their passage. They pushed on hard, and when one of the men got tired, he'd simply ride on the sled until he'd gotten his breath back.

It was full winter now. An unrelieved whiteness stretched away in every direction. Raider wondered how the hunters could find their direction, but by early afternoon they had reached the dwelling where the unpleasant white man was reputed to be staying.

Raider and Sergeant Stuart held a brief council of war. Simply rushing inside the house and facing Whiskey Joe, if it was indeed him, was not an appealing prospect. One of them would have to crawl up that tunnel-like entranceway, with the man they were after above and partially out of sight. Not an appealing prospect.

They sent in the English-speaking hunter. As an Inuit,

he was not likely to arouse Whiskey Joe's suspicions. As the man crawled into the entranceway, Raider and Sergeant Stuart stepped back out of sight, rifles ready. Sergeant Stuart laid a warning hand on Raider's arm. "Remember, I want him alive."

"After what he's done?" Raider asked, remembering the slaughtered Indians, and remembering also his treatment at Whiskey Joe's hands.

Sergeant Stuart nodded affirmatively. "That's the way we do it here. That's my duty. We bring our men back alive, so they can have a fair trial. If we can."

Yeah. If we can, Raider thought to himself.

Both men stiffened as they saw a figure show itself in the entranceway. It was the hunter. He stood up, brushing snow off his parka, then walked over to Sergeant Stuart. The ensuing conversation was in such broken English that Raider could not follow it, but apparently Sergeant Stuart could. He thanked the man and turned toward Raider. "The white man isn't here any longer. It seems that his behavior grew so bad—something about his abusing a girl—that the people here made him leave. Threw him out into the cold to die, which was fine as far as they were concerned. They're damned friendly people, but they will not take abuse. So... out with whoever it was. As far as I can figure, he left only a couple of hours ago."

"Do they know which way he headed?"

"Yes. West. He'll probably try and make it to Tuktoyaktuk."

"How's he armed? Do they know?"

"Yes. They took away his rifle but let him keep his pistol."

"Better and better. Let's get on his trail. Damn! I think we got him!"

Sergeant Stuart nodded. A few minutes later they were off, the dogs yipping wildly, Sergeant Stuart steering, the other men running alongside the sled.

They pushed on hard, wanting very much to catch their quarry before dark fell. This time of year the days were quite short, providing only a few hours of rather dim light. There were still a couple of hours of light left, so they easily picked up the man's tracks leading away from the Inuit dwelling, the rather pathetic tracks of a single man, alone in this vast frozen landscape. In this part of the world, being alone in the wintertime was usually synonymous with death. Exile was the worst possible punishment, reserved for those who broke the all-important harmony of Inuit life, those who interfered with the intricate web of cooperation without which the entire group would perish.

They came in sight of their quarry a little before dark, showing up as a solitary speck, black against the snow. When they had gotten to within a third of a mile, the man apparently heard the dogs. They could see him spin around, hold still for a moment, then turn and begin to run.

He could never outdistance them in this vast open space, not while they had the dog sled. Which the fugitive quickly proceeded to take away from them. He had been traveling along the coast, about a hundred yards from the sea. The pack ice reared up on his right, cracked and faulted by the vast weight of ice behind, all of it pushing up against the land. The fugitive swerved, leaped up onto a jagged, tilted ice floe, then disappeared from sight.

"Damn," Sergeant Stuart said quietly. He raced the dog team toward the spot where the fugitive had disappeared, the others following. Reaching the edge of the floe, he jumped down from the sled. "Come on, let's leave the dogs here and get after him."

Raider and two Inuit followed him up onto the floe. One man stayed behind to care for the dogs. "Be careful," Sergeant Stuart warned. "He could be anywhere... and he's got a pistol."

Raider nodded and checked his rifle. He had already jacked a round into the chamber—not that it would necessarily fire. He'd had to be careful with the rifle; the icy air was capable of freezing the action solid, making it unusable. He'd done his best to avoid that by keeping the action close to his body.

The footing on the ice was treacherous. Great crevasses yawned. Towers of cracked and tortured ice rose on all sides. "There he is!" Sergeant Stuart suddenly shouted.

Only about fifty yards ahead, a figure had darted out from behind a chunk of ice. His hand held a dark object. "Hit the dirt!" Raider shouted, forgetting that there was no dirt to hit, only ice, and it jabbed at his body as he ducked low. A second later the short flat sound of a pistol shot rang out, bouncing back and forth against the ice, followed almost immediately by a second shot. Ice chips flew into the air where the bullets struck.

Raider cautiously stuck his head around a corner. "Throw down your gun, Devlin, and come out with your hands up. You can't get away."

There was a moment's silence, followed by a stream of obscenities. "Raider! You son of a bitch! Is that you out there?"

It was definitely Whiskey Joe's voice. "Sure as hell is," Raider shouted back. "Now do like I said. Come on out with your hands in the air."

More cursing. "Go fuck yourself, Raider. I shoulda killed you when I had the chance."

"You got that right, old son."

Sergeant Stuart cut in, calling out, "This is Sergeant Douglas Stuart of the Northwest Mounted Police. Throw down that gun. Give yourself up before it's too late."

"Too late for that, Mountie. I know damned well that if you take me back I'll hang, so if you want me, come on and get me."

Raider and Sergeant Stuart glanced at one another, nodded, then began to move forward, one at a time, moving from cover to cover, each man taking his turn covering the other. The Inuit followed a little farther behind, wary of the gunfire but grinning with excitement.

Whiskey Joe fired several more times, accurately enough to force his pursuers to advance cautiously. Raider fired twice, the heavy bullets of his Centennial chipping big chunks of ice very close to Whiskey Joe's head, mak-

THE NORTHWEST RAILROAD WAR 183

ing the fugitive cry out in fright and anger and duck back out of sight.

After fifteen minutes of hide and seek they finally felt they had him cornered. There was a gap in the ice pack behind where Whiskey Joe was hiding, a hundred-yard stretch of open, freezing water. Whiskey Joe had moved into what Raider suspected would be his last defensive position, behind an uptilted plate of ice. The problem was, how were they going to close in on him? A lot of open ice lay out in front of Whiskey Joe's cover. He'd pick them off if they tried to make it across.

Raider and Sergeant Stuart were huddled together, trying to formulate a plan, when they heard Whiskey Joe utter a terrible cry, followed a moment later by a thunderous, inhuman roar.

Both men leaped to their feet and started toward the big uptilted piece of ice. More roars were coming from behind the ice, accompanied by Whiskey Joe's screams, now screams of agony.

Whiskey Joe suddenly appeared around the edge of the ice, stumbling, screaming, bloody. Instantly, an enormous mountain of white fur followed around the outcropping, reached out a massive paw bristling with huge curved claws, and dragged him back.

"Polar bear!" Sergeant Stuart shouted. He raised his rifle to his shoulder but could not shoot; Whiskey Joe was too entwined with the bear. The huge animal was mauling him, chewing on the top of his head. Whiskey Joe's parka was red with his own blood.

Whiskey Joe struggled partway free, which gave the bear enough space to seize Whiskey Joe's arm in its jaws. The bear, snarling and roaring, tore with its jaws while shoving with its paws, and to the horror of the observers, one of Whiskey Joe's arms came away in the bear's jaws.

The bear was on Whiskey Joe immediately, tossing away the bloody arm and once again seizing its victim in a bear hug. Sergeant Stuart thought he saw his chance. He raised his rifle to his shoulder, ready to try a desperate shot, when he was suddenly pushed from the side so that his shot went wild.

He spun, expecting to see Raider, but it was one of the Inuit who had spoiled his aim, the one who spoke English. "Not do it!" the man said sternly. "Too late to save man, bad to kill bear."

Sergeant Stuart subsided. In the lexicon of the Arctic, where nothing was to be wasted, the man was right. Whiskey Joe was already as good as dead. Better that he be left to feed the bear, which someday might furnish a meal for hungry Inuit.

The bear, up on its hind legs, towering perhaps nine feet into the air, had lifted Whiskey Joe off the ice. Its massive jaws settled around his victim's head, grated against bone, then with one savage bite crushed Whiskey Joe's skull. Whiskey Joe's legs shuddered, and his last agonized scream floated out over the ice pack.

It now became important to get the hell out of the area. The bear had seen them, and, having dropped Whiskey Joe's body, was making short rushes in their direction. Raider at first thought the animal was loath to leave its kill, but then one of the Inuit called out and pointed. A large white ball of fur had come around the edge of the ice, a cub. "He musta run into the cub," Raider called out to Sergeant Stuart. "Mommy came to the rescue."

The men slowly moved backward, never taking their eyes off the bear. It continued its rushes, but was not eager to get too far away from its cub. Finally, the men were off the ice pack and heading for the dogs, all of whom were creating a terrible uproar. They had smelled the bear.

Neither Raider nor Sergeant Stuart said much for the first hour of the return trip. It was Sergeant Stuart who finally broke the silence. "I feel that I've failed. Not only did I fail to bring my man back, but I left his body back there . . . to be eaten."

Raider slowly shook his head. "Ah hell, you didn't fail at all. Anyhow, what you just said was egotistical as hell."

"What the hell do you mean by that?" Sergeant Stuart demanded, his anger flaring.

"Come on, Sergeant. Think. Why the hell are you so anxious to bring a man back, anyhow? It's for justice, isn't it? The word is justice."

"Well, yes. Of course."

Raider shrugged. "Fine. What we saw was justice. But it wasn't men, or the law, or courts that laid out the justice. It was something... well, something bigger."

"You mean... God?"

"Well, I dunno if that cuts much ice with me, thinkin' of it like that, all that stuff about the old man with the long gray beard. But think about it. What's the worst thing you feel Whiskey Joe ever did? His worst crime?"

Sergeant Stuart thought a moment. "When he killed all those Indians a couple of months back."

"Well, there it is. There it was, I mean—the bear. Lots of Indians think of the bear as a sacred animal. That white monster that took Whiskey Joe looked godlike as hell to me. That bear was the Indians' animal, and Whiskey Joe's crimes were mostly against Indians, so... I kinda think it was those Indians that got justice."

Sergeant Stuart rode on silently for a while. "Well," he finally said, "it sure feels a hell of a lot better to think of it that way, doesn't it?"

"Yep. Sure does."

The hard-hitting, gun-slinging Pride of the Pinkertons is riding solo in this new action-packed series.

J.D. HARDIN'S
RAIDER

Sharpshooting Pinkertons Doc and Raider are legends in their own time, taking care of outlaws that the local sheriffs can't handle. Doc has decided to settle down and now Raider takes on the nastiest vermin the Old West has to offer single-handedly...charming the ladies along the way

__0-425-10757-4	**TIMBER WAR #10**	$2.75
__0-425-10851-1	**SILVER CITY AMBUSH #11**	$2.75
__0-425-10890-2	**THE NORTHWEST RAILROAD WAR** #12 (On sale June '88)	$2.95
__0-425-10936-4	**THE MADMAN'S BLADE #13** (On sale July '88)	$2.95

Please send the titles I've checked above. Mail orders to:

BERKLEY PUBLISHING GROUP
390 Murray Hill Pkwy., Dept. B
East Rutherford, NJ 07073

NAME_____
ADDRESS_____
CITY_____
STATE_____ZIP_____

Please allow 6 weeks for delivery.
Prices are subject to change without notice.

POSTAGE & HANDLING:
$1.00 for one book, $.25 for each additional. Do not exceed $3.50.

BOOK TOTAL $_____
SHIPPING & HANDLING $_____
APPLICABLE SALES TAX $_____
(CA, NJ, NY, PA)
TOTAL AMOUNT DUE $_____
PAYABLE IN US FUNDS.
(No cash orders accepted.)

MEET STRINGER MacKAIL
NEWSMAN, GUNMAN, LADIES' MAN.

LOU CAMERON'S
STRINGER

"STRINGER's the hardest ridin,' hardest fightin' and hardest lovin' hombre I've had the pleasure of encountering in quite a while."
—Tabor Evans, author of the LONGARM series

It's the dawn of the twentieth century and the Old West is drawing to a close. But for Stringer MacKail, the shooting's just begun.

_0-441-79064-X	STRINGER	$2.75
_0-441-79022-4	STRINGER ON DEAD MAN'S RANGE #2	$2.75
_0-441-79074-7	STRINGER ON THE ASSASSINS' TRAIL #3	$2.75
_0-441-79078-X	STRINGER AND THE HANGMAN'S RODEO #4	$2.75
_1-55773-010-5	STRINGER AND THE WILD BUNCH #5	$2.75
_1-55773-028-8	STRINGER AND THE HANGING JUDGE #6	$2.75
_1-55773-051-2	STRINGER IN TOMBSTONE #7 (On sale July '88)	$2.75

Please send the titles I've checked above. Mail orders to:

BERKLEY PUBLISHING GROUP
390 Murray Hill Pkwy., Dept. B
East Rutherford, NJ 07073

NAME_____
ADDRESS_____
CITY_____
STATE_____ ZIP_____

Please allow 6 weeks for delivery.
Prices are subject to change without notice.

POSTAGE & HANDLING:
$1.00 for one book, $.25 for each additional. Do not exceed $3.50.

BOOK TOTAL $_____
SHIPPING & HANDLING $_____
APPLICABLE SALES TAX $_____
(CA, NJ, NY, PA)
TOTAL AMOUNT DUE $_____
PAYABLE IN US FUNDS.
(No cash orders accepted.)